COUNTRY AT HEART

The Blazing Eagle Ranch 3

PEYTON BANKS

✿ I ✿

"**D**on't let anyone make you do nothing you don't want to do." The firm words came from someone she highly respected.

Demi Day sat in the comfy oversized chair that overlooked the grounds of the home she was currently renting. The wall was made completely of floor-to-ceiling glass, allowing her to have the full effect of the yard. The family room was outfitted with plenty of couches, a feature fireplace she could almost stand up tall in, plush carpeting, and entertainment center decked out with an eighty-inch smart television.

But none of those held her attention today.

It was the serene nature outside her window that garnered her attention.

"I know they can't force me to sign a new contract," Demi murmured. "They are worried that I will sign with another label."

Her friend, confidante, and mentor, was none other than Nina Hunt, legendary R&B singer.

Demi was an up-and-coming singer who Nina had taken under her wing. Her current contract was up, and the record executives were hounding Demi. She had a deadline when the papers needed to be signed.

"Take your time. There are plenty of options in this day and age. When I first started, I wasn't so lucky," Nina said.

Demi nodded, even though she knew Nina couldn't see her. The woman was a genius, and Demi was absorbing everything she could. The two women had grown close over the years.

"The main reason I hesitated is because I want to do a country album. This has been on my mind and on my heart for a while now, and they won't hear of it," Demi spat.

Hell, she was from Texas.

Country-western music was in her blood.

She'd grown up listening to her father's records.

Charley Pride, Aaron Neville, and George Strait were some of his favorites.

"Why won't they?" Nina asked.

"Because of the demographics that follow me and buy my music won't cross over." Demi rubbed her face, the frustration she had felt in the meeting with the executive rushing back to her.

"Is that so?" Nina snorted. "Well, when I wanted to do an album on my own, I just did it. Released it independently."

"I can't do what you did." Demi laughed. "You broke the damn internet with that album."

Demi remembered that day as if it were yesterday. It had been all over the news and social media that Nina Hunt had dropped a secret album. All of the online retailers crashed from fans trying to purchase and download the record.

Demi had been so happy for someone she now considered a sister. At the time, Demi was recording her first album and had recently met Nina. They were label mates and ran into each other. They quickly hit it off and became fast friends.

Which was shocking to Demi since Nina was such a mega pop star, but she was down to earth and willing to help Demi achieve success.

"But I took back my creative control and did what I wanted. You see it paid off."

That it did.

Her album titled *Nina* went diamond, selling over fifteen million copies.

Demi turned her attention back to the large window by her. The beautiful landscape meeting her was just what she needed.

Calm, serene, and beautiful.

Right in the middle of the country.

She'd found the home for rent in the town of Shady Springs, Colorado, located forty miles south of Colorado Springs.

With all of the pressures building up on her, she needed a break. Somewhere she could escape, and Shady Springs proved to be that place.

It was filled with plenty of country air, open spaces, and that small-town feel that was channeling the country girl in her.

"How do I do that?" Determination filled Demi. The record executives did not always know what was best. Branching out to do what was in her heart was what being an artist was about. She needed to grow as a person in order for her creativity to blossom.

"That's what I'm here for, sis," Nina said softly. "The suits want to be able to make all the money they can from you. They will drain you and not give two shits. This would be your chance to take control of your own destiny. There's no one who can tell you what to do when you release an independent album."

"This is sounding too good to be true." Demi sighed.

"Do you want to be forever tied to the label or have more freedom like me?"

Demi chewed on her lip while she thought of the question. Of course, she wanted to be like Nina. She basically idolized the woman. Her business sense was like nothing Demi had ever seen before.

"If so, then I will have my lawyers meet with you and help curate a deal like mine. I'm here for you, Demi."

Demi's vision blurred. Meeting Nina had been very intimidating. She was the largest rock star on the planet, and she had made Demi feel as if they were best friends from the start. Nina was all about empowering her fellow black women.

"Let's do it," Demi whispered.

Nina's squeal echoed in her ears. She grinned, ready to take control of her life.

It was just all too much at the same time, and she was glad she had Nina in her corner. All of her life, she had wanted to share the gift of her voice with the world. She'd never thought in a million years she'd be in the predicament she was in.

To be a famous pop star, be able to travel all over the world to perform, provide for her family in ways she only could have imagined… Demi was still not used to it.

But not only did she have to worry about renewing her record deal, she had something else in the works.

One of the largest cosmetic companies had made her an offer she couldn't refuse. Their aim was for her to not only be the face of a new exclusive line, but it would be hers and she had control on products and got a hefty chunk of the profit. They wanted to tap the market of ethnic hair and skin.

The amount of money she was set to make from this was mind-boggling.

Life was going amazingly well.

"Well, I will be in touch. Love you, sis." Nina giggled.

"Thanks, Nina. Love you, too, sis."

They disconnected the call, and Demi sat frozen in her chair.

Who would have thought a little country

bumpkin from Texas was going to get to have the world at her feet?

Demi lost track of how long she sat staring out the window. There was so much on her mind she hadn't heard her sister and nephew walk into the room.

"Earth to Demi." Jaimie snapped her finger and thumb in front of Demi's face.

Demi blinked and saw her elder sister laughing at her. Jaimie fell down on the couch and tucked her feet underneath her.

"Auntie Demi. How did you not hear us?" Hakim laughed. He was an eleven-year-old who had stolen Demi's heart from the moment she'd first seen him in her sister's arms after he was born.

"I was just lost in thought." She chuckled. "This scenery is just so beautiful, and I was taking it all in."

She focused on Jaimie who was studying her closely. If anyone could read her, it would be her sister. With Hakim in the room, Demi knew Jaimie would wait to ask her about it when they were alone.

"Auntie, we are in the middle of nowhere." Hakim groaned. He flopped down on the floor by his mother's feet.

Demi giggled watching him roll on the floor playfully.

"Are there any kids my age I can play with?"

He was shy kid, really, and had dealt with some major bullying in school. Jaimie had made the hard choice to pull him from traditional school and home-school him.

He loved traveling with them, so at the insistence of Demi, she offered to pay for tutors to help with his schoolwork.

Jaimie Day was a proud, independent single mother and at first refused.

But with as much as she had done for Demi, there was no way Demi was going to allow her to refuse.

It was the least she could do, and she loved her nephew as if he were her own son.

"Maybe we can reach out to the local school district and see, babe." Jaimie grabbed his foot and tickled him.

He screeched and crawled away from her, grinning.

"What do you want to do today?" Demi asked, turning her attention to her sister.

"Well, the tutor will be here within the hour.

Why don't we go into town and grab lunch?" Jaimie shrugged.

They had been in town a short while and were still learning the layout. Demi had rented the home for a few months, and they had plenty of time to stay. If she needed to go back to LA or New York, she'd just fly out there.

For now, they were going to be living in the country.

"No fair. I want to go." Hakim pushed up off the floor with his legs folded.

"Sorry, little boy. You have school to do," Jaimie teased.

He rolled his eyes, muttering.

"How about this. Your mom and I will go out for lunch, and tomorrow I'll take us out to dinner. Your pick."

"But I don't know anywhere around here. There's nothing but cows." He sighed.

"You tell me the type of food and I'll find it," Demi promised. She leaned forward and held her hand out for him to shake. "Deal?"

"Barbecue." He didn't even hesitate to place his hand in hers.

"Well, we're not in Texas anymore, but I'm sure we can find somewhere here that does a mean barbecue. There are enough ranches around, I'm sure someone has to." Demi laughed.

They were originally from Waco, Texas, but once Demi had made it big, her sister had immediately taken the job as her manager. She'd left her high-paid job as a regional sales director for a major corporation to work with Demi. It was risky for her, but it worked out immensely.

"I'm sure there has to be," Jaimie agreed. "Okay, bud. Go put some clothes on. Miss Summer will be here soon."

"Yes, Momma." Hakim stood and rushed out of the room.

Jaimie's gaze followed him before landing on Demi.

"Spill it."

Demi chuckled and shifted in her seat. She brushed her hair from her face and gazed at the ceiling. The wood beams were her favorite feature in the room.

"You always know when something is bothering me." She sighed.

"Well, not only am I your sister, but I'm your manager, and I know we have some important things to discuss."

Jaimie hit her with a serious look, and Demi knew Jaimie had on her manager hat right now.

"We do. I just got off the phone with Nina, and she offered me some great advice."

"And what is that?"

"I go independent."

Jaimie stared at her and nodded. "I actually agree."

"What? You do?" Demi hadn't expected her to be on board immediately. She had assumed she was going to have to talk her into it, show her numbers, and prove why it would be a good move for her.

"You can control everything about your brand, your sound, it makes complete sense." Jaimie stood from the couch and paced. "Plenty of artists are making this move. This allows you to even bring home more money. The label makes more money off you than what you bring home. Why let the man get richer off of you?"

"That's basically what Nina said," Demi murmured. She was beginning to grow excited about the notion.

"Oh, my goodness, Demi." Jaimie paused and faced her with a wide grin. "You can record the country album you've always wanted to do, and with the cosmetic contract, you are going to be swimming in dough. The world will be your playground."

Demi jumped up and rushed her sister. They hugged, screamed, and jumped around.

Her life was falling into place like she'd always dreamed.

"Okay, let's go out for lunch. We have so much to discuss," Demi said, pulling away from Jaimie. "I also hear there are some nice shops and restaurants downtown."

"I also hear there's a ranch that specializes in working with kids and offers riding lessons. I want to look into that."

They walked out of the family room and headed toward the stairs.

"You know the name of it?" Demi asked.

"The Blazing Eagle Ranch."

$\maltese$ 2 $\maltese$

"**T**hank God they are having a good ol' country wedding," Carson muttered. "If I had to wear a tuxedo, I was going to have to have a serious chat with our soon-to-be sister-in-law."

Carson Brooks shuddered just thinking of the penguin suit.

"This is one way we know Maddy and Parker were meant to be together." Wade chuckled. He slapped Carson on the back, walking past him.

Carson grinned thinking of his eldest brother. Parker and Maddy were finally getting married. It was many years in the making, one kid already and a baby on the way, and Carson couldn't be happier for them.

The road to marriage had been rough for them. Their conniving father had blocked their path to happiness, and it hadn't been until Maddy moved back home that light was shed on the entire situation.

Now, the two of them were madly in love, and Parker was going to make an honest woman of Maddy.

Carson shook his head. His brothers were settling down, and he was the only single one.

Wade would be the next one to get hitched. He had popped the big question to their longtime neighbor, Joy. Their relationship had been a rocky one since their families had been rivals. But now that Joy and Wade were going to be tying the knot and welcoming their first child, all was well between the two families.

He wouldn't admit it, but he was kind of jealous. Parker and Wade had found women who could not only put up with their stubborn ways but love them unconditionally.

None of the Brooks men were perfect.

Secretly, Carson yearned for what they had. He wanted a good woman by his side and a little Brooks running around.

He loved his nephew, Tyler, like his own, but then again, there was nothing like a child of his own.

Carson sent up a prayer that his turn would be next.

He moved over to the shirt section. Smith and Sons was a popular men's apparel store located in Shady Springs. He and his brothers frequented it when they were looking for some new clothes.

The Brooks brothers were as close as siblings could be. Carson was the youngest of the three. Parker was the one who'd protected him and Wade from their father's wrath once their mother had died. Carson had been in junior high when his mother passed away from lung cancer.

Not ever had Grace Brooks smoked a cigarette.

But lung cancer swooped in and took her from them.

Their father was a bastard before she'd died; afterwards, he'd unraveled.

And Parker was there as a buffer between the old man and them.

Jonah Brooks loved his boys in his own way, but he sure had one hell of a way of showing it.

Carson pulled out a crisp white button-down shirt with a blue design on the back.

"What do you think of this?" He held it up for Wade to see.

His brother glanced away from the belts he was browsing and squinted at the shirt.

"Isn't it tradition that only the bride wears white?" Wade snorted.

"What? You mean a man can't wear a white shirt to a wedding?" Carson laughed.

"Hell, I don't know. When was the last time we went to a wedding?"

Carson blinked, unable to recall the last wedding he'd gone to. He grinned. His football buddy from college had got married a few years ago, but that was a destination wedding on the beach of St. Thomas where the dress code was swim trunks only.

"All right. I'll play it safe," he muttered. He put it back and picked another one that was navy blue. "How about this one?"

Wade nodded. "That's a good color."

His brother headed into the changing room with a few items in his hands.

This was proving to be easier than Carson thought, holding on to the shirt. He moved along and decided to find a new pair of jeans.

He finally chose a pair, then glanced around the store. This was a special occasion, maybe he should get new boots. If his mother were alive, she'd fuss about new clothes and old shoes.

A smile came to his lips at the memory of his first junior high dance. She'd taken him out shopping, excited for him. There was a girl he'd had his eye on, and she'd wanted to make sure he looked his best.

"What do you think?" Wade's voice cut into his memories.

Carson walked over to where his brother stood, checking himself out in front of the full-length mirror.

He'd chosen a pair of black jeans and a solid red button-down shirt.

"It would seem like shacking up has added a few pounds to your middle," Carson joked.

Not really. They were in the best shape they could be, thanks to the physical labor of running a ranch.

"Like hell." Wade snorted.

He put up his fist, playfully swinging at Carson who blocked the soft blow with one hand. Wade stepped forward, launching his other fist.

"Don't make me put these clothes down," Carson warned.

"It wouldn't do you any good." Wade snickered.

It was good to be out with his brother. Life on the ranch had been hectic lately, and the Brooks siblings hadn't hung out in a while.

Carson sort of missed them. He saw them just about every day, but it wasn't the same as before their women had come into their lives.

Not that Carson didn't like Maddy and Joy, they were great, but deep down he knew it was him being the youngest and wanting all of the attention.

Growing up, his brothers had always taken care of him. The three of them played football in high school, but it was Carson who'd gone to college on a football scholarship.

His brothers were his biggest fans.

Jonah loved the fact he hadn't had to shell out money for college and had gone to a few games, but it was Wade and Parker who'd ensured he'd trained and stayed in top physical shape on the off seasons.

Carson had offers to go professional, but that life had never interested him. He had used that full ride to get a fancy degree that was collecting dust on his wall. His degree was in business, and it had helped with the family ranch.

His father used him to work with the meat-packing companies to strike up the deals. Carson had a way with him, that he was able to bend companies to his will and get them the best deals possible.

Jonah knew what he was doing. He always ensured each son was involved with the family business for when it was time for them to take over the reins so it would be an easy transition.

"You fellas finding everything to your liking?" Neil, the store's manager, strolled over to them with a wide grin on his face.

"I think so." Carson lightly shoved Wade away from him. Holding up the outfit he'd found, he spun around toward Neil. "Wade over here doesn't believe he's gained a little weight."

"Ass." Wade slapped him on the back of his head.

"Watch it." Carson chuckled. He turned his attention back to Neil. "How's the family? I heard your wife had the baby."

"Yes, Shannon did amazing." Neil pulled his cell phone from his pocket, sharing pictures of his daughter. He was a beaming father, showing off his new pride and joy. "This is Emily."

"She's beautiful," Wade murmured. Envy was beaming brightly in his eyes.

Carson inhaled, happy for his brothers. Both of them would be able to be the father theirs wasn't.

The Brooks brothers would be wiping the slate clean.

Parker had been amazing with Tyler. They had become the best of friends, always together. It was scary how much Tyler was like Parker.

Carson promised he would be just as attentive and involved in his children's lives as Parker was in Tyler's.

Neil ushered them to the register, ringing them up. The manager of the store made sure they had everything they would need for their brother's big day.

Carson wasn't sure how he ended up with a new belt and a cap along with the other items he'd picked out.

"Neil is one hell of a salesman." Carson laughed, staring down at his bags.

They headed toward Wade's truck parked in front of the store.

"Nothing wrong with splurging once in a while." Wade shrugged.

They tossed the bags in the back seat and hopped in the vehicle.

"Wanna grab a bite to eat?" Wade asked.

"I'm starving. Let's go over to the Notorious COW."

Wade pulled the truck out of the parking lot and headed to the barbecue joint. They arrived a few minutes later and entered the restaurant.

The lobby was packed.

"I guess everyone decided to grab lunch here today." Wade sighed.

"I'll ask about the wait." Carson navigated his way through the small crowd and arrived in front of the hostess. She was a pretty young girl. Carson turned on the Brooks charm and offered her a wide grin.

"Hey, there. How long of a wait?" He narrowed his eyes on her, watching her blush. Carson knew the effect he had on members of the opposite sex. He wasn't above using what the good Lord had blessed him with to get a table at the barbecue place.

"Um, hi." She glanced down at the screen then met his gaze again. "It's going to be about forty to fifty minutes."

Carson's smile vanished. His stomach grumbled. There was no way he was going to make it to fifty minutes.

"Go ahead and put my name down for two." He tossed her a wink, laughing as her blush deepened.

"Carson for two," she murmured.

He hid his surprise that she knew who he was.

"Gotcha."

"Thanks." He backed away and found his brother leaning against the wall in the corner. He moved back over to Wade and let out a sigh. "Forty- to fifty-minute wait."

"What? Why is so many people here?" Wade glanced around the waiting area. "I guess we can see how long it will take. Are you in a rush?"

"Not really." Carson moved closer to his brother to allow a couple to brush past them.

The door opened, and two women entered the lobby. One was tall, slim, with short black hair. The second one trailing behind her was shorter, curvy, with long hair and huge sunglasses that pretty much took up her entire face.

Carson's gaze wouldn't leave her. He found himself needing to see her eyes.

They walked over to the hostess, speaking with her.

"Anyone you know?" Wade nudged him.

"Not that I'm aware of." Carson shook his head. "She looks familiar, but I can't place her."

As if feeling him staring at her, the shorter one turned and took in the room. Her attention landed on him. She offered a smile; her perfect white teeth sparkled.

His heart skipped a beat.

She was downright gorgeous.

"You're staring," Wade murmured.

Carson blinked and turned to his brother.

"Why don't we run over to the Tipsy Cow and grab lunch there," Carson suggested. He ran his hand through his thick hair. His stomach grumbled again, protesting at how long it was taking for them to be seated.

"They won't have a wait time," Wade agreed.

"Excuse me," a soft voice said.

Carson felt a tug on is arm. He turned and found the pretty brown-skinned woman with the large glasses standing at his side.

"Hello." He grinned.

She was much shorter than him and had to tilt her head back to meet his eyes. She pushed her sunglasses up to rest on top of her head. Her eyes were almond-shaped and the prettiest deep-brown shade he'd ever seen.

She was a knockout.

He had the feeling he'd seen her before but couldn't put a finger on it. If he had met her previously, there was no way he'd forget her.

"We're new to town," she announced.

Her friend came to stand by her.

"Welcome to Shady Springs." Carson held his hand out for her.

She placed her smaller one in his, giving him a firm shake.

"I'm Carson, and this is my brother, Wade."

"Demi, and this is my sister, Jaimie." Demi returned his smile. "I didn't mean to eavesdrop, but I heard you say there was somewhere that wouldn't have a wait. We were curious and are starving."

The girls laughed, but it was Demi's that drew Carson to her. Deep down inside, he knew he wanted to hear her laughter again. It was musical, and he wanted to be the reason for her smile and laughter.

"There's a bar not far from here called the Tipsy Cow. It's about five minutes away," Wade shared.

"You're welcome to follow us over there," Carson suggested. They shared a look between the two of them. "I promise you the food is good."

"Lead the way, cowboys." Demi winked.

CARSON HELD OPEN THE DOOR TO THE TIPSY Cow for Demi and Jaimie. Wade tailed him inside the bar.

Carson bit back a snort. It had been a while since they had been allowed to come into the Tipsy Cow after the night Parker had got into a fight with Billy over Maddy.

Carson met the gaze of Jerry, the manager, who returned Carson's smile with a scowl.

"Ladies, if you want, we can sit over at the bar." Carson waved them to follow him and Wade over.

Maddy was working the bar. Her belly was enormous. If Parker hadn't told them it was only one baby inside, Carson would have assumed she was pregnant with twins.

"My two favorite brothers-in-law," Maddy greeted them with a wide grin.

"Hey, Maddy. You're looking beautiful as always." Wade chuckled, taking a seat at the bar.

"You're just saying that because your brother knocked me up." Maddy rolled her eyes. "What brings you guys here? I didn't think Jerry would allow you in."

Carson's ears warmed.

"Don't worry about it. We have an agreement with Jerry," Carson admitted. He turned and waved Demi and Jaimie to the chairs next to the one he was standing in front of. "Maddy, this is Demi and Jaimie. Maddy's our soon-to-be sister-in-law."

"Hello. Nice to meet you." Demi removed her sunglasses, pushing them back to the top of her head.

Carson pulled both chairs out for them, assisting the girls to their seats.

"Oh, my goodness." Maddy froze in place, staring at Demi. Soon a squeal escaped from her, and she jumped in place, her gaze never leaving Demi.

"What is wrong with you, woman? Are you in labor?" Carson scratched his head. He'd always assumed labor would be screaming and pain, not grinning and hopping around in place like a goof. Even the cows screamed and moaned when birthing their calves.

"Carson, do you know who she is?" Maddy shrieked.

Carson glanced at his brother who shared his confusion.

"Nope. Not a clue," he admitted sheepishly. "Should I?"

Demi was chuckling while Jaimie bit her lip, apparently trying to keep from laughing at them.

Maddy leaned crossed the counter to whisper loudly, "Carson! I only play her music like every day. It's Demi Day!"

He blinked.

He did recognize the name. Maddy was right. Lately, anytime he stopped by the house, she had her music on blast. She called it nesting while cleaning and driving his brother crazy. Parker had shared with him and Wade that she had been purging the house and getting it ready for the baby.

"Oh," Carson replied.

The girls fell into a fit of giggles. He and Wade just shrugged and let them have their fun.

"I actually think it was cute how you didn't know who I was," Demi said, wiping the tears from her face. "I knew it the moment I approached you in the other restaurant. I figured you were safe to follow since you were so clueless."

"Most people recognize my sister immediately. That's why we're here in Shady Springs, just to get away," Jaimie said.

"Welcome to Shady Springs," Maddy said, her wide grin still in place. "You will find this town to be laid-back and a great place to relax or have a good time."

"It may be a small town, but there's a little of everything you can do here," Wade chimed in.

"Thank you." Demi smiled and tucked her hair behind her ear. "I've missed small towns and I'm looking forward to everything it has to offer."

"Here are the menus. Go ahead and look at them. What can I get you to drink?" Maddy asked the sisters.

"What about us?" Carson sputtered. Maddy had completely ignored him and Wade.

"I already know what you two are going to order." Maddy rolled her eyes again.

"I don't know. Maybe I'll want something different," Wade drawled.

"Really?" Maddy rested her hands on her hips. She snagged two menus and slid them to Carson and Wade. "Both of you order the bacon cheeseburgers, a portion of wings, and loaded fries with a Coke."

"Damn, that would go straight to my hips," Demi murmured and reviewed the menu.

Carson's gaze dropped down to her hips, and he bit back a retort.

She was perfect as she was. Curvy and full-figured.

Just like he liked his women.

"The Brooks men can eat whatever they want and still don't gain a pound." Maddy sighed. She rubbed her belly. "I live with two of them, and even my ten-year-old can never eat enough."

"I always need fuel for all the hard work I put in." Carson laughed. He mimicked Maddy, rubbing his washboard abdomen. She was right, but with all of the physical labor that was required from running a ranch, they burned through the calories they consumed.

"You know what?" Wade interrupted. He glanced up from his menu and shrugged. "I'll just have the usual."

"Me, too." Carson grinned.

Maddy glared at them as if she was scolding Tyler.

"Don't give us your 'Mom' look." Wade snickered.

"We'll have the same, but me and my sister will split one order of wings," Demi said.

"Extra pickles on my burger," Jaimie chimed in.

Maddy wrote their orders down and took back the menus. She appeared to be happy, and Parker was head over heels in love with her. Carson wasn't sure why Maddy was still holding on to her job at the bar, and he wasn't going to ask. Parker had warned him he'd lost the battle when it came to her working outside the home. The Brooks family owned one of the largest cattle ranches in the state.

"I'll be right back with your drinks." She waddled away, singing a song off-key.

"Wait, did she say your last name was Brooks?"

Jaimie swung her chair to face them. "As in the Blazing Eagle Ranch?"

"The one and only," Wade murmured.

"We were asking around about riding lessons for kids and we were told to call you." Jaimie smiled.

Wade went on about the ranch and Kiddie Camp. It was his pride and joy, and he could speak about it for hours on end.

Carson took the time to study Demi while Wade held her attention. She was beautiful, and he didn't care who she was.

He wanted to get to know her better.

"Kiddie Camp is normally held in the summer," Wade announced.

Carson nudged him slightly. He wanted to have a reason for her to come to the ranch and he wasn't above using her nephew as an excuse.

"But if you are looking for something for your son while you are staying here in Shady Springs, we'd be more than welcome to help," Wade said.

"Would you?" Demi gasped. "Hakim would love this. He's been dying to learn to ride and find kids his age while we are here."

Maddy returned with their drinks, dispersing them. She glanced over at Jaimie. "How old is your son?"

"Eleven," Jaimie replied.

"Tyler is soon to be eleven. I'm sure he would love to meet your son. We can arrange a play date if you like," Maddy suggested.

Jaimie and Demi nodded simultaneously.

"He's been dying to meet someone his age. Hanging with Mom and Auntie gets old fast." Demi chuckled.

"If you like, I can teach you how to ride a horse if you are up to it," Carson offered and turned his attention to Demi.

"I think that would be nice." She smiled and took a sip of her soda.

"That does sound like fun," Jaimie said. She stood from her chair. "Excuse me. Where's the restroom?" she asked Maddy, who gave her directions.

"Did I hear someone say you're getting married?" Demi asked Maddy.

"Yes." Maddy sighed, getting a dreamy look in er eyes. "It's going to be a good ol' country wedding outdoors. The barn is going to be decorated nice, music, fall air. I can't wait."

"A fiancé meeting you at the altar, too." Carson chuckled. She'd mentioned everything about the wedding except his brother.

"Of course he'd be there, silly." Maddy grinned.

"Sounds amazing. It's been a while since I went to a down-home wedding. The last couple I went to were expensive Hollywood ones," Demi said.

Carson's eyebrows rose.

"Why don't you come with me?" he blurted out.

Maddy and Demi slowly focused their attention on him. Even Wade's eyebrows rose sharply.

"I couldn't." Demi gasped.

"I don't have a plus-one." He shrugged. "And you want to experience everything small-town while you are here in Shady Springs."

"I don't want to just invite myself." Demi turned and looked at Maddy. Her teeth snagged her bottom lip.

Carson couldn't take his eyes off her plump lip. He wanted to pull it away from her teeth and replace it with his.

"Oh, my goodness. It would be an honor to have you at my wedding." Maddy grinned, hopping up and down in place.

Demi swung her chair around to face him. Her smile widened as she met his gaze.

"Sounds like it's a date."

Demi couldn't remember the last time she'd laughed so hard. Wade and Carson were a riot. Both of them were extremely handsome. She couldn't imagine seeing the three of them together. Their family had downright good genes.

Wade, they learned, was engaged to a sheep farmer, but Carson was single.

Demi had a hard time looking away from his steel-gray eyes. The crows' feet surrounding them showed he smiled a lot. It had been a long time since she had met someone who just enjoyed her company.

They were caught up in sharing stories from their youth.

"So Carson and Parker were getting chased by the sheriff's department." Wade laughed. He slapped his brother on the shoulder. "They had hopped the fence to old man Graham's ranch so they could go cow tipping."

"Oh my! And the police were after you?" Demi giggled.

"Hell, yeah. We tried to outrun them on foot. Mr. Graham called the police saying that we were trying to steal cows." Carson scoffed. "Like, we have a ton of them. What do we need to steal one for?"

"The police chased them with their blue-and-red lights on." Wade elbowed Carson. "Finally caught them, too. Put them in the back of the squad car and took them home."

"What did your parents say?" Jaimie's eyes grew wide.

Demi already knew her sister was dreading the rebellion teen years with Hakim. He was a good kid, and Demi was sure they wouldn't have anything to worry about with him. But hearing these stories, it would be hilarious if Hakim got into trouble like this.

Not that her sister would find it funny.

"When Pa looked at us, I thought it was going to be the end of days for us." Carson snorted.

He took a sip of his drink. His eyes crinkled in the corners with his smile. He turned his attention to her, and if Demi were crazy, she'd say her heart skipped a beat.

Those damn gray eyes of his.

She bit her lip and stared into them.

"Did you get in trouble?" Demi cleared her throat, surprised at the huskiness in her voice.

"He put us to work so bad on the ranch for two weeks straight that every muscle in my body hurt. It was worse than football training." Carson shook his head, grimacing.

"You played football?" Demi asked. It certainly explained his size. Her gaze roamed him, taking him in. He was a few inches over six foot which was a weakness of hers. His brown hair was thick, and he kept running his fingers through it to push it away from his face. Her fingers itched to touch it.

What was she doing?

Demi blinked.

Here he was being friendly with her and her sister, and she was eyeing him like he was a juicy steak.

"Will you look at the time," Jaimie announced. "Time sure passes by fast when you're having fun. Hakim should be done with his tutor."

Demi had to hold back a pout. She wasn't ready to leave. She looked down and saw that their food was all gone. They had sat around talking and laughing.

It felt good to be normal.

"The offer still stands." Carson turned those big gray eyes on her.

She noticed a slight dimpling in his cheeks and knew she was captivated.

She was single, staying in Shady Springs for a while.

She needed a break from the limelight...why couldn't it include riding a cowboy?

"I'd love to go with you." Demi wasn't going to pass up the chance to spend a day with the sexy rancher.

"Then if that is the case, you're going to need this." He reached over, snagged a pen from the counter, and a napkin. He scribbled something on it before handing it to her with a wide grin. "Now, this is a private line directly to me. Anything you need, I'm just a call away," he drawled.

His wink had her clenching her legs together.

"Oh, my goodness. This is the most important napkin ever," she joked, holding it up to her chest. "I shall protect it with my life."

With dramatic flair, she folded it and tucked it away in her purse.

Jaimie and Wade chuckled at their display.

"Here, let me get the check," Demi offered. She stood and opened her purse.

"No need, superstar. Already taken care of." Carson chuckled.

"Oh, well thanks." She eyed her sister who nodded. She must have missed him paying for their lunch.

"No problem at all." He stood near her, and the scent of his cologne was intriguing.

She wanted to lean in close and sniff him.

He might be turned off by a woman randomly leaning in and breathing him in.

It had been a while since she had dated someone not in the industry, and suddenly she didn't know what would be considered the 'norm.'

"Thanks for stopping by," Maddy said, rushing over to them as fast as her belly would allow.

"The food was so good. Please give my compliments to the chef," Jaimie said.

"I will! He'll be pleased to know newcomers enjoyed his food." Maddy laughed.

"I can't wait to see you at your wedding. I'm so excited." Demi was already thinking of what she could wear to the event. This was the first time she wouldn't have to be dressed by some fancy designer and could just wear what she wanted.

"It's an honor to have you there." Maddy grinned. She pointed to Carson. "If you get this one to behave, I will seriously love you forever."

"What? Just me?" Carson sputtered.

"You know how you Brooks brothers are." Maddy rolled her eyes. A customer sat down at the end of the counter. "I'll see you boys later."

With a wave, she waddled away to take care of her new diner.

Demi and Jaimie walked out of the bar with Carson behind her. Demi had the feeling he wasn't ready to part from her either. Wade headed toward their truck parked a few spots away from their rental. Jaimie scurried away also, as if sensing Demi wanted a few seconds alone with Carson.

The strolled together in a comfortable silence, stealing looks at each other.

Their eyes met, and they burst out in laughter.

"You can come out to the ranch at any time," Carson offered. "I wouldn't mind giving you an official Shady Springs welcome, country style."

They arrived at the passenger door of the car. Demi leaned against it and tilted her head back so she could meet his gaze. His eyes darkened, and she was captivated by the heated stare.

He was interested.

The way his gaze traveled along her body, she hadn't had anyone truly see her for a while, and it was an amazing feeling to have.

Her breath caught in her throat.

She was used to people telling her she was beautiful, but for some strange reason, what Carson thought mattered.

He was genuine.

Nothing was fake about him.

Anything he was sure to say, would be the absolute truth.

"Well, as long as you are giving me a private tour of what Shady Springs has to offer, I'd be interested."

A panty-melting smile spread across his face.

If Demi didn't have jeans on, her panties would be engulfed in flames and around her ankles.

"Don't worry your pretty little head, superstar." Carson's country drawled thickened. "I'll be your personal tour guide for as long as you are here." He opened the door and helped her into the vehicle. "Y'all have a great day."

He shut the door and walked over to his brother's truck. Demi settled in and put her seat belt on as Jaimie pulled out of the parking spot and drove off.

"You little hussy," Jaimie teased.

"What?" Demi tried to act innocent. She immediately thought of the napkin tucked away in her purse. She was going to have to transfer his number into her cell phone when they got home.

"He's sweet on you."

Demi grinned. "You think?"

"Girl, neither one of you were ready to leave. You were practically pouting."

"I was not." Demi nudged Jaimie with her elbow. She paused, frowning. "Oh, no."

"What is it?"

"What about you? I got so caught up in the wedding I didn't think about you. I'll call them—"

"It's okay. I don't have to go. Plus, I'm making plans with Hakim."

"You sure?" Demi felt horrible for forgetting about her sister.

"I'm fine. Don't worry." Jaimie waved her hand. "I wouldn't want to be a third wheel anyway."

"Okay."

"You are not in town a week and already you are picking up men." Jaimie shook her head.

Demi watched the scenery go by and realized that

Shady Springs may have been the best decision she'd made in a long while.

"Now don't forget why we are here," Jaimie said softly.

Demi grew quiet.

The tone in her sister's voice was that of her manager. "We are here not for men, but soul-searching and career decisions that need to be made."

"I know." Demi scoffed. "I'm the one who planned this trip."

She tried to push down her attitude. She had been all work for years, and it had paid off.

Who got to make a decision about a multimillion-dollar record deal and a cosmetic line that could make her worth jump up to a half a billion dollars?

It was a lot of pressure on her shoulders. The recording industry was brutal and didn't care about her or anyone aside from the money they could make off of their artists.

Leaving the record label and going independent? It was a risk, and she was going to take it.

With Nina's guidance, she couldn't go wrong.

If she wanted to relax and live a little. Didn't she have that right?

AFTER CHANGING HER CLOTHES TO something more comfortable, Demi made her way to her office. They had returned home with Jaimie going to check on Hakim.

She couldn't shake the butterfly feeling in her stomach.

Carson's gray eyes and sexy grin were still on her mind.

She glanced down at her phone in her hand and smiled. Carson's number was officially in her contact list.

Now, she had to try to keep herself from calling him.

The office was located in the back of the house and overlooked the yard. There were plenty of luscious green trees that provided privacy. There was a brick patio where the family could chill, grill out, and a hot tub.

Demi loved everything about the home. It had everything she wanted and needed to escape the city life.

She padded inside and closed the door behind her. She took a seat at the desk and opened her laptop to plow through her emails. There were so many waiting for her that it was going to take her a while to get through them all.

Her attention was caught by one from her lawyer. His email highlighted the potential contract Adore Me cosmetics was offering. She skimmed through it, and it was okay, but if they wanted her face to be the forefront, they needed to ensure she was paid more.

She responded to the email with her terms. The backend royalties needed to be priced a little higher. They were still in the negotiating phase, and she wanted to have more say so on product placing and direction of the brand.

Makeup had been her passion growing up. Her mother, Emma, was a makeup artist who got her start working at the makeup counters at department stores. She then moved on to become one of the top makeup artists in their town of Waco, Texas. Demi and Jaimie were always her test subjects. They would play for hours with the makeup and allow their mother to put on a full face for them for practice.

Finished with her requests, she reread what she'd typed before sending the email out.

A shaky breath escaped her.

It was ballsy, but it was business. They were going to make a killing off her and her brand, why couldn't she do the same from them?

She eyed the rest of the emails and didn't see any that jumped out as important. She really didn't feel like going through them.

She'd allow Jaimie to do it as her manager.

Instead, she pulled up a new browser and searched for something cute and fun to wear to an outdoor country wedding. It was next weekend, and she had to make sure what she wore caught a certain cowboy's attention.

❧ 4 ☙

The scenery of the Blazing Eagle Ranch flew by. Carson knew the lay of the land like the back of his hand.

It was his family's legacy.

The sky was bright blue and not a cloud in sight. It was an abnormally warm fall day, and Carson wasn't going to complain. This week was going to be perfect weather for ranching, and the weekend was going to be even better for a wedding.

Parker and Maddy were going to have a beautiful day to tie the knot.

Carson guided his SUV along the road that led to his father's home. He pulled up to the house and parked. Killing the engine, he stepped from the vehicle and gazed at his childhood home.

There were plenty of memories, good and bad.

Carson walked toward the house as Tom, his father's physician/therapist, came out of the house. He was a lanky man, dressed in black scrubs. His hair was riddled with gray, and his face was full of wrinkles. He came highly recommended from the hospital and had been able to put up with Jonah, so that was saying a lot.

"Hey, Carson. You're right on time," Tom called out.

Carson jogged up the stairs and took Tom's hand in a solid shake.

"Is that so?" Carson asked.

"I think we are at a good point where I can discharge Jonah from therapy," Tom said, stepping back. "He's doing amazing and has made much improvement since I first started working with him. He should be fine."

"That's great news." Carson folded his arms in front of his chest.

"Jonah will need to keep working out, and soon he should be back to his normal self. I left some papers on the table in the kitchen for suggested workouts."

"He don't need workouts," Carson joked. "We'll

throw him back out on the ranch. That will whip him into shape."

"That will certainly build muscle." Tom chuckled. "Take care of him."

"Will do." Carson gave Tom a small salute, watching the therapist jog down the stairs and head toward his car.

Carson entered the house. It was the home he and his brothers had been raised in. He could remember the days when he was a kid and his mother was alive. The house always smelled of her cooking and baking. That woman had been a goddess in the kitchen.

Without Grace Brooks, it just wasn't a home any longer.

Once the boys were grown, they hadn't wanted to move back in with Jonah Brooks, the patriarch of the family. He was a tough son of a bitch.

Always had been.

Grace had been what grounded the old man.

Life around the Brooks homestead had taken a turn for the worse when Grace had died.

Jonah had taken her death hard and practically forgot about the boys for a while.

Thankfully, Parker was there to step up and ensure Wade and Carson were looked after.

The boys were rambunctious and got into tons of trouble.

The sheriff's department had made frequent trips to their homes.

They were almost like a cab service for the Brooks brothers, and they had a standing tab down at the office.

At least twice a month, Jonah had to bail if not one, but all the boys out.

The Brooks brothers never started fights, but they were very proficient at ending them. Carson grinned thinking of the last time he and his brothers got into a barroom fight.

The smile slowly faded with the memory of Wade drinking too much. That night, Carson would have sworn he'd aged a few years.

Wade had alcohol poisoning and had been sent to the hospital from jail. The deputies didn't want him dying in their cell.

Carson could still remember trying to wake his brother.

They had been inside a cell together while waiting for their father to come bail them out yet again.

Carson hadn't shared with his siblings, but he

had been left with nightmares from the fear he would lose his brother.

Carson rested his head back along the stone wall and blew out a deep breath. Parker stood by the barred doors of the jail, glancing out into the hallway.

"Pa is going to be pissed." Carson chuckled.

Parker snorted. Wade was abnormally silent.

Carson turned his attention to his brother and found him slumped in the corner.

"Wade?" he called out.

Wade didn't move.

"Someone can't hold his liquor in his old age." Carson snickered. He slid along the bench next to Wade and slapped his leg. "Wake up, sleeping beauty."

Nothing.

His grin slowly faded as Wade didn't even flinch.

"What's wrong?" Parker glanced over his shoulder.

"He's not waking up."

Parker walked over and took Wade by the shoulder and shook him. Wade's head rolled to the side.

"Fuck," Parker cursed.

Carson flew from his seat and raced to the bars. Fear took hold of him. They couldn't let anything happen to Wade.

"Help!" Carson yelled out. "We need help over here!"

Davis and his boys were in another cell. They stood near

the entrance to their cell with curiosity on their faces. It had been their fault that all of them were locked up. Davis, Joy's brother, had started the fight over Wade dating Joy.

Parker slid Wade's body to the floor and turned his head to the side.

A deputy came jogging down the hall. "What the hell are you yelling for?"

"My brother is unconscious, and we can't get him to wake up," Carson said.

The deputy took one look at Parker on the floor with Wade and radioed for backup. He opened the cell and rushed inside.

Carson ran a hand over his face as he watched the deputy check Wade for a pulse. Another deputy sprinted inside, on the radio calling for an ambulance.

Wade's body jerked, vomit spewing from his lips.

Guilt filled Carson.

He had known they were going too hard at the festival.

Wade and Joy had broken up, and he had wanted to drown his sorrows that night.

He should have watched his brother closer.

Everything passed by in slow motion. The EMTs arrived after what seemed forever. Wade had vomited twice by the time they had come into the cell.

Carson and Parker had been released from jail not too much longer than Wade being whisked to the hospital.

The wait in the hospital had been torturous. Carson and Parker had never been so scared before. Just thinking Wade may not make it was not an option. It was always the three of them.

Hours later, Wade finally woke up.

CARSON WALKED ALONGSIDE HIS FATHER TO the barn. Jonah was determined for them to go riding together. There was no way in hell Carson was allowing the old man to go by himself.

Jonah was an ornery son of a bitch, but that didn't mean Carson wanted harm to come to him.

"I'm sure Twister has missed you," Carson said.

Jonah had had Twister for the past ten years, and the horse's personality matched that of his owner.

"I hope y'all have been taking care of my boy." Jonah's voice was raspy.

They entered the barn and headed to where Twister and Carson's horse, Tucker, were kept.

"We have," Carson replied.

He took notice that Jonah was moving much better. He no longer used his cane and wasn't hunched over. He stood tall and walked with a steady gait. He was coming around and had better coloring.

Jonah had been fit for his age before the heart attack.

"Good."

Carson's gaze dropped down to Jonah's gut. It was more pronounced than it usually was.

"Looks like you're getting a little potbelly there, Pop. Eliana's cooking must agree with you," Carson joked.

"That's why I need to get back to work and out of the house," Jonah grumbled. "I swear that woman is trying to fatten me up like a Thanksgiving turkey."

Carson barked a laugh. He and his brothers knew Eliana was sweet on their father.

It had to be the only reason she'd stayed on as long as she had. Most of the other nurses at first hadn't lasted a week.

Eliana had blown into their lives and handled Jonah, allowing the brothers to concentrate on running the ranch.

They worked on getting their horses prepped, saddles on. They walked next to each other, guiding the horses out of the barn. Carson stayed near his father, wanting to be near him as he prepared to mount Twister.

"If you come over here and spot me like I'm some

damn child, I'll tear you a new hole." Jonah glared at him.

Carson grinned, holding up his hands. He backed away and moved toward Tucker.

"I just wanted to make sure—"

"I've been riding horses long before you were born, boy. I know how to get on my horse." His father growled.

"Hey, Tucker, boy. Let's go ride with Pa and Twister." Carson rubbed Tucker's neck before swinging up on him. He shifted in the saddle until he was comfortable.

His father did the same. Some things just didn't leave a man who'd been riding horses as long as he could walk.

They trotted around the barn and took off east.

"Anything in particular you want to see?" Carson asked after a few minutes of riding.

"I want to see the herd." Jonah led the way.

They had just rotated the cattle to a new pasture. Carson wasn't going to ask his father why he wanted to see the cows. It was their family business, and Jonah would want to take a look at what put money in their pockets.

They rode in silence until they arrived at the destination. Jonah brought Twister to a halt. Carson stopped Tucker near them and paused. Jonah's gaze roamed the area.

"I want you to drive up to Greely and speak with BBFS," Jonah announced, breaking the silence.

BBFS was the Better Beef Food Service, one of the leading processors of beef in the state. It wasn't too out of the ordinary for Jonah to ask him to negotiate for the family business.

"Sure, I can do that."

"They want to put in an order, and from the size they are asking, it would be best if you went in person." Jonah eyed him.

Jonah always wanted to put his fancy business degree to work. Carson was fine with that. It gave him purpose with the ranch. Each of the boys had things they were best at, and negotiating deals in the meat industry was right up Carson's alley.

When Jonah officially retired, Carson and his brothers would be granted equal rights as partners of the Blazing Eagle Ranch.

It was their inheritance.

This land had been in their blood. From the moment they each could walk, it was on Brooks land.

"Not a problem, Pa. I'll take care of it," Carson assured him. He didn't mind the traveling and representing his family's business. It gave him a chance to get away and pull his weight on the ranch. He had some ideas that one day he would sit down and speak with his brothers about.

Carson wanted to ensure that not only would his children be taken care of because of the Blazing Eagle, he wanted to make sure that his grandchildren and their children would carry on the family legacy.

The Blazing Eagle was one of the largest cattle ranches in the state, and they prided themselves on the good quality meat they were able to produce. They were going to have another great birthing next year.

Carson could feel it in his bones.

They fell quiet, both of them lost in the beauty of the open country before them. He would love to show Demi around. Her beautiful smile came to mind.

She was downright gorgeous.

He couldn't believe he hadn't recognized her.

But then again, on television she would be dressed up, tons of makeup, but yesterday had showed a fresh face.

Au naturel.

The woman didn't need makeup.

It should be a crime to put anything on her face.

He was curious why she'd chosen Shady Springs to hide away. He wondered where she was from.

She had the slightest hint of a twang when she spoke. He hoped she called him.

Carson Brooks had never got stood up before for a date.

The wedding was this weekend, and he would be damned if he showed up alone. He should have got her number.

Carson's gaze landed on his father. He wasn't sure what had transpired between Jonah, Parker, and Maddy, but all they knew was that Jonah was going to be in attendance at the wedding.

That reminded him that he needed to speak with Parker. There was no way in hell he was bringing it up with his father.

He already knew what his father was going to say.

None of your damn business, boy.

But Carson was curious.

Jonah had done something awful that had kept Parker and Maddy apart.

Had they forgiven him?

"Have y'all checked on the haying equipment?" Jonah asked.

"Yes, sir. Tomorrow I had planned to work on

them. Me and Karl will set to work on oiling and performing maintenance on all the machines. First cut should be done this week."

"Well, sounds like I've taught you boys well." Jonah slapped Carson on the shoulder. "This ranch is running like a well-oiled machine."

Carson's eyes grew wide. That was the biggest compliment Jonah had ever given him.

Usually, Jonah was full of snarky retorts. Sarcastic comments or backhand compliments.

But never one as nice was what he'd just said.

"Thanks, Pa. That means a lot. We just always wanted to make you proud." Carson tried not to get choked up. He stared at his father as if seeing him for the first time. This was a new Jonah, and Carson was afraid if he blinked the old Jonah would return.

He glanced away at the sound of hooves on the ground. Karl and Darnell were headed their way.

"You boys have. I know I haven't always said it, but you have. I'm sure your ma is smiling down from Heaven at you boys. Even with all the shit y'all got into, you turned out to be fine men." Jonah pushed off the fence and walked toward the hands, leaving Carson frozen in place with his mouth wide open.

❧ 5 ❧

emi had performed in front of thousands of screaming fans. Today, she didn't know why she would be so nervous.

She'd never experienced this before.

Her heart was racing.

Normally before a performance she'd have little butterflies that disappeared the second she stepped out onto the stage.

Now, she sat with her legs folded on her massive king-sized bed and stared down at her phone.

The napkin Carson had written his number on was resting on the mattress.

She'd entered the number in her contacts, but for some reason she couldn't bring herself to throw away the napkin.

"You can do this." She blew out a deep breath.

For at least ten minutes, she'd been trying to get the courage to call him. It had been two days since she'd seen him.

Hell, she had ordered her dress that should be delivered today.

Dammit, just do it, Demi.

She scooped up her cell and dialed his number.

"Now or never. Now or never." She sighed.

"Hello?"

His deep baritone voice came onto the line, sending tremors down her spine. Goodness, this man's voice was the sexiest thing she'd heard in a long while.

"Hi, is this Carson?" She bit her lip. Like it would be anyone else answering his phone, but she would be polite.

"You got him," he replied.

"It's Demi." Her pulse thundered in her ears. She inhaled sharply, trying to draw breath into her lungs.

"Demi, the superstar," he murmured.

The sound of her name on his tongue had her falling back against her plush pillows. She squeezed her thighs together, growing aroused by his voice alone.

Demi closed her eyes tightly, a smile playing on her lips.

"No, just Demi, the woman on vacation."

"I'm just playing with you, girl." He chuckled. "I hope you aren't calling to cancel our date."

"For the wedding? No, I'm coming. I wouldn't do that to Maddy."

"Oh, but me you would be okay ditching?"

She burst out laughing. He had a way about him that just kept her grinning. His laughter echoed in her ears.

"I'm sure there is some gal standing off in the shadows waiting for her chance with Carson Brooks," she teased.

He was a very good-looking man. Those gray eyes, thick brown hair, and muscular frame were sure to pull all the women. Without even asking, Demi was convinced there were some broken hearts out there.

"If there was, then she missed out. I got my eyes on you, Demi," he said softly.

Demi squeezed her eyes shut again.

What was it about this man?

"Talking like that, I might show up to the Blazing Eagle Ranch on a whim," she threatened playfully.

"Well, you never know. I might be crazy and give you the directions now," he retorted. "I live for craziness."

She giggled and rolled over onto her side. Her eyes connected with the window revealing the gorgeous morning sky. The entire wall was a row of glass that allowed the sun to filter in while showcasing the stunning view of the country. There was a balcony off the master suite that held a small dinette set where she had taken to drinking her coffee and writing.

So far, they had gotten lucky with the weather this week. Shady Springs was turning out to be the perfect location for what she needed.

Open skies, fresh air, plenty of space, and good-looking cowboys.

Realizing the time, she wondered what he had been up to.

"I didn't wake you?" she asked. She checked the clock on the bedside table, seeing it was a little after eight in the morning.

"I'll have you know that when you were snoring your little heart out—"

"I don't snore," Demi interjected with a snort.

"I'm sorry, when you were daintily sawing logs, I

was up at five in the morning drinking my coffee and heading out to the barn," he said.

"Five in the morning? Hmmm…correction. I was rolling over in this big ol' bed," she replied haughtily.

He barked a laugh. "I'm sure you were beautiful turning over."

She loved the sound of his laugh. It was wholesome and not fake. She smiled. This was something she needed. In her line of business, there were only few people she could trust to be honest with her. Most people in the entertainment industry were faker than acrylic nails.

"Well, when you look as good as me, it can't be helped," she joshed.

"Don't we all have that problem?"

She sighed. He, of course, probably looked like he had just stepped out of one of those fitness model magazines when he woke up. He was a rancher, and doing physical labor all day gave him a natural physique. It also didn't help that the man used to play football, and his size gave that away without her even asking.

He was tall and built.

Her thoughts wandered to what he would look like without his flannel shirt.

Was there a sprinkle of hair on his chest? Or was it bare? What if he was completely covered in soft hair?

She heated up just thinking about it.

Demi needed to change her train of thought before she combusted.

Get a grip, girl.

"So how about it?" he asked.

"What?" She blinked. She must have daydreamed too long and missed what he'd said.

"Why don't I give you my address and you come by? I'll give you a tour of the ranch."

Demi bit her lip. Hakim was already excited about visiting the ranch and getting his own invite.

"Bring your sister and nephew," Carson suggested as if sensing her hesitation.

"Okay, we'll come," she blurted out. Who was she kidding? She wanted to spend time with this man and would not miss out a chance.

"Great. Is this your cell phone number? I'll text the address to you."

"It is. Give me about two hours?"

"That'll be fine. Can't wait to see you."

They disconnected the call. Demi dropped her phone on the bed beside her. She stared at the ceiling. The recessed ceilings were beautiful and were one of the things that had caught her eye about the house. Aside from the gorgeous Colorado skies and land.

Her heart was still pounding, and she found herself grinning from ear to ear.

Carson.

She blinked.

What she was feeling was something she needed to write down. She rolled over and grabbed her notebook and pen from the nightstand drawer.

Standing from the bed, she had to get this down on paper. She padded across the room and went out onto the balcony. She sat on a cushioned chaise.

Opening the notebook, she turned to a blank page. Her pen flew across the pages as a song presented itself.

A certain cowboy who could make her smile came to mind.

She inhaled and allowed her creativity to flow.

Those gray eyes.

Make me want to do things.

A good country gal don't talk about it.

She shows you what's on her mind.

Wrap those strong arms around me.

Hold on, cowboy.

We're going for a ride.

She grinned, thinking of her conversation with Nina. The woman was right. It was high time she took control of her destiny.

She could be whatever she wanted to be, and at the moment, she wanted to do what she wanted.

Today, it would be to go visit her cowboy and enjoy life.

"WHO CALLED WHO?" JAIMIE ASKED.

Demi rolled her eyes. Of course, her sister wanted all the details. Demi focused her attention on the road, tightening her grip on the steering wheel.

They were on their way to the ranch. Carson had texted her the address and directions to ensure she didn't get lost.

This morning, she'd written the first song for her country album. She didn't have a title for the album, but the song, *Her Cowboy*, would definitely be included. Nina had texted her the meeting details with the lawyers. Demi was growing excited about this. She would have never thought in a million years she'd be contemplating releasing independently, but if other artists could do it with music, books, and movies, then she could, too.

She had the best mentor a girl could ask for. There's no way she could fail.

"I called him," she admitted sheepishly.

"You hussy!" Jaimie laughed, nudging her with her elbow.

"What was I supposed to do?" Demi shrugged. She wasn't ashamed that she'd called him. Their conversation had left a smile on her face all morning. "I didn't give him my number, so it was in my ballpark. At least I didn't call him the same day."

"I'm surprised you didn't. The way you two were making googly eyes at each other, I totally expected you to."

"Really?" Demi scoffed. Did she appear that thirsty for a man's attention?

"I mean, it's been a while since I've seen you so genuinely interested in someone who made you smile. It was actually cute."

Demi glanced in the back seat and found Hakim engrossed in his video game system in his hands. His earphones were in his ears.

"You know how it is. Most men in the industry, or trying to get in the industry, say they like me but really have an agenda to see if dating me will boost their career," she said dryly. That was why she rarely dated. It was hard to distinguish who really wanted to be with her versus those who wanted to use her.

"I know. I'm just busting your balls." Jaimie sat back and stared out the window.

"You did give me a speech the other day," Demi reminded her sister. The GPS system on the dashboard advised her to turn at the upcoming road. She slowed the car and followed the instructions.

"I know, but then I got to thinking of everything that happened that day. Seeing you like that made me happy, sis."

Demi glanced at her. "Thanks, sis."

"You never know. We might find love here in Shady Springs."

Demi's eyebrows jerked up high. "We?"

"Hey, you're not the only one who can look at all of these hot cowboys." Jaimie snorted.

They fell into a fit of giggles. Jaimie had been hurt by Hakim's father. The idiot had run as soon as he had heard Jaimie was pregnant. He had tried to come back around once he'd seen Demi make it big.

He had figured he could ride her coattails since Jaimie was her manager.

He was a deadbeat, and after plenty of drama and a restraining order, he'd finally left Jaimie and Hakim alone.

They didn't need anything from him. Demi ensured Jaimie and her nephew were well taken care of.

If her sister felt she was ready to start looking for love, then Demi would be right there with her, cheering her on.

Both of them deserved to have someone in their life who made them smile, feel safe and loved.

Shady Springs was a beautiful town. The country scenery passing by was picturesque and could be featured on the front of magazines.

"Well, here's to us both finding love," Demi declared.

"Hear, hear." Jaimie held out her fist.

Demi met it with hers. They grinned at each other, sealing an unspeakable deal between them.

It was time for them to find love.

The GPS system announced the next direction: "Right turn, five hundred feet ahead."

Soon the turn came, and an overhead sign announced Blazing Eagle Ranch.

"Wow," Demi murmured. She took in everything around them as she guided the car down the dirt road. Her heart sped up with the thought of seeing Carson again.

She had never been forward before in pursuing a man.

There was a first time for everything.

Demi Day was going after her sexy cowboy. She wanted to get to know him and everything there was that made up Carson Brooks.

The big, sexy rancher better watch out.

This superstar always got what she wanted.

$$\text{✻} \quad 6 \quad \text{✻}$$

"Dammit," Carson cursed. He snatched back his hand and immediately saw a line of blood. "Fuck."

He pushed back from the tractor's engine and reached for the towel sitting on the edge of the machine. He wrapped his finger and squeezed it to stop the flow of blood.

"You good?" Karl asked, lifting his head from the other tractor he was working on.

Karl Tanis had been a hand on the ranch for some years. He'd moved to Shady Springs from a few towns over, looking for a better paying job. He came highly recommended from his old boss, and Parker had no issues hiring the hand on full time.

Karl had grown up working ranches. His dark hair and fit physique had the ladies always latching on to him whenever they all went out. Karl had a great personality and was an easy-going guy. He was in his mid-thirties and still had yet to settle down.

Carson snorted.

He wasn't even thirty and already he was trying to find that special someone. Maybe his father's ranting about them settling down had taken or it was the fact that his brothers and friends were all finding their other halves.

Karl was just living life and enjoying every bit of it.

They were trying to get the tractors tuned up smoothly. They were getting prepared for hay cutting. Carson had hoped they would have them running today so they would be ready bright and early tomorrow.

"Want me to take over?" Karl moved over to him.

"Nah, I'll be fine." Carson unwrapped his finger and took a peek at the cut. "It's already stopped bleeding."

It wasn't the first time he'd cut his hand working on their machines. He tossed the rag back down and picked up the wrench.

Karl shrugged and went back over to his tractor.

Carson got back to work. He had promised his father they would be ready.

Music blared out from the speakers in the building. They were in the working barn where they kept a lot of the farming equipment. Carson had outfitted the structure when he was younger.

If he was going to be out here working, he at least wanted to jam to his favorite music. The building had grown hot. There was no AC, no wind blowing through. The sun was high and beaming down outside.

Sweat ran down his back. He'd taken his shirt off, not wanting it to get soaked or streaked with grease.

It was always a bitch to get out on laundry day.

Carson tapped his foot to the beat of the song. He was almost done with this tractor. He just needed to replace the spark plugs and the fuel filter, then this baby was going to purr.

He stepped back, dropping the wrench down where the other tools sat. He tugged his bandana from his back pocket, running it along his forehead and hair.

It was about eighty today so far, but in the barn, it felt a little under Hell.

They were experiencing an Indian summer, and he wasn't going to complain. Replacing the bandana in his back pocket, he went to find the things he needed to finish up the tractor. He had to hurry.

A certain brown-skinned songstress was going to be visiting soon.

He wanted to be able to devote some time to showing her and her family around the Blazing Eagle.

"This one should be ready," Karl announced. It was the tractor Wade had purchased at an auction.

"Really?" Carson pulled the items he needed from the shelves where he kept parts around. He walked back and stopped near the tractor Karl had finished.

"This baby wasn't in bad shape. There wasn't much to do." Karl slammed the hood down. He strode around and hopped in, starting it. The engine roared to life. The sound was smooth.

"Well, alrighty then." Carson grinned and continued on with his. He rushed through the job so he could ensure his would be fine, too.

"Carson!"

He turned at the sound of Parker calling him. He glanced over his shoulder and saw his eldest brother marching toward him with a curious look on his face.

Carson's gaze immediately landed on Demi ambling alongside Parker. His mouth went dry at how gorgeous she was. Her long dark hair was braided across the front while the rest was left down. She wore shorts and a shirt that stopped above her navel. His eyes were drawn to the small jewelry on her belly button.

His cock twitched.

Her feet were encased in sandals.

"Demi and Jaimie." He grinned, standing to his full height. Finishing off the tractor was easily forgotten. He'd have Karl test it out and ensure it ran.

Carson snagged his shirt from the hook on the wall and threw it on. He walked over to them, buttoning it up. Demi's assessment of him didn't go unnoticed. Heat flared in her eyes as she traced her gaze along his body.

Carson bit back a chuckle.

He already knew what he looked like.

Football and ranching were hard work, and his body was proof of it. He took pride in his appearance, and from her expression, she was appreciating it. Their eyes connected, and she glanced away, biting her lip.

Busted.

Carson grinned even wider.

"Hello," the girls echoed.

"I'm assuming my brother introduced himself." Carson arrived in front of them. "Demi and Jaimie, this is Karl." He pointed to his friend behind him.

Karl shut off the tractor and hopped down. He, too, was without a shirt. He waved to the girls and moved over to the machine Carson had been working on. Jaimie's gaze lingered on the hand before flicking away.

"Hello." The girls waved to Karl, then their attention changed back to Carson.

"And who do we have here?" Carson's gaze landed on the kid who was taller than Demi and her sister.

"This is my nephew, Hakim." Demi rested her hand on his shoulder and brought him ahead of her.

"Nice to meet you, Hakim." Carson stepped forward and took his hand in a shake. He seemed shy and quiet and appeared to be the same age as Tyler.

"Hello, sir." Hakim looked him in the eye. There

was a resemblance between him, his mother, and aunt.

"They are visiting Shady Springs for a while, and I offered to show them the Blazing Eagle," Carson shared, glancing over at Parker.

"That was nice of you." Parker smirked. He turned to Demi, his smile widening. "My fiancée called me screaming about meeting some star at her bar. I'm to understand that was you?"

"Yeah." Demi grinned. "I thought she was going to go into labor or something."

"Not before the wedding." Parker groaned.

"I don't see why y'all just didn't go to the court-house and get married." Carson shrugged. "Then we could have cut straight to the party."

"Were you going to be the one to tell Maddy she couldn't have the wedding of her dreams?" Parker's eyebrows rose.

Carson thought of his sister-in-law and her pregnancy mood swings.

"Yeah, I'm not that brave." Carson shook his head.

Laughter filled the air.

"I better be going. Nice meeting you." Parker tipped his hat to them. He walked past Carson, slapping him on the back. "If you see my son, send him my way."

"Will do." Carson chuckled. His nephew had become a master of hiding from his parents.

"He's with Wade and Rashad," Karl called out from inside the barn. "Dr. Hutson is checking out a couple of the geldings."

"You all want to go see the vet check out the horses?" Carson asked. Dr. Hutson was always a star with the kids. "I can introduce you to my nephew. That will give you someone to hang out with who's your age."

It brought a smile to Hakim's face.

"That would be cool," he said.

"I'm sure hanging with older women isn't fun," Carson joked.

"Hey." Demi swatted his arm.

He had searched online to learn more about her. He had been curious about who she was. He wasn't familiar with the genre of music she sang. He was more of a country and blues man. According to what he had found, she was a couple of years older than him.

"I just meant from the perspective of a child, older people aren't as fun to hang with," Carson tried to clean it up. He motioned for them to follow him. Carson rested an arm around Hakim's shoulders. "Now, when you are my age, older women are extremely fun."

"Wait a minute!" Jaimie burst out laughing. "He's not dating until he's at least twenty-five."

Carson winked at Hakim who fully grinned back at him. Carson glanced back to the women.

"Look, he's going to figure it out on his own." Carson sighed, shaking his head. "Personally, I don't mind a woman being older than me." He wagged his eyebrows at Demi over his shoulder.

She bashfully turned away, but he didn't miss her smile.

They arrived at the barn where Wade, Rashad, and Tyler were with Dr. Hutson. They had one of the brown geldings outside the building. Dr. Hutson was examining its mouth.

Carson quickly introduced everyone. Tyler immediately perked up at the sight of Hakim. Tyler was a Brooks and not shy at all.

"Hey, I'm Tyler," he said, stopping by Hakim and offering his hand.

"I'm Hakim." Hakim took Tyler's outstretched hand.

"You want to see the abscess?" Dr. Hutson asked.

The boys glanced at each other, smiles forming

on their faces. They raced over to the doctor. The horse was a calm one, allowing them to peer inside his mouth. The kids were captivated by the physician as he spoke.

"I want to start treating him with an antibiotic first to see if just some medicine will help him out," the doctor explained. "I really don't want to pull a tooth if I don't have to."

"That would be fine," Wade said. "We can do the medication first."

"I need to assess the pregnant mare also before I leave." Dr. Hutson pulled out a vial from his bag and drew up medication in a syringe. He motioned for the boys to watch him administer the shot of antibiotics.

Within minutes, Rashad was leading the gelding back into the barn.

"Mom, can I go with the doctor to check on the pregnant horse?" Hakim asked.

"I want to see a pregnant horse, too." Jaimie laughed, excitement on her face. "I'm going to tag along with the boys."

The group walked away with the vet to the corral where the pregnant mare was grazing.

Carson turned to Demi.

His heart skipped a beat.

"Looks like it's me and you," he said, unable to take his eyes off her.

"I hope you're not scared of being alone with this old woman," Demi said.

Carson's face warmed slightly. She hadn't told him her age when they had met the other day. He glanced around, combing his fingers through his hair.

"Okay, so I'll admit I Googled you."

Demi giggled, staring at him. He held out his arm, allowing her to slide hers around his. Carson led them away from the barn.

He finally had her to himself. Demi had been on his mind since the day they had met. She leaned into him, reminding him of how much smaller she was compared to him. He could easily rest his chin on the top of her head.

"You know you shouldn't believe everything you find on the internet."

"True, but I will have to say there are some interesting pictures."

"I don't even want to know which ones you saw." Demi covered her face, a groan escaping her lips.

He laughed at her embarrassment. For someone who was as popular as she was, he would think she would be stuck up, or unapproachable. Instead, she was the complete opposite.

"Someone of your status, I would have thought you'd have bodyguards to roll with you." He'd always imagined that celebrities had protection details with them when they traveled.

"I do, but I didn't want them here. If I need them, they are a call away," she admitted. She scanned the land.

Carson tried to see it from her eyes. He took pride in his homestead. This land was his family's legacy and handiwork.

"But that is why I wanted to get away to a small town. I can just be me," she said.

"Well, you don't have to worry about anyone messing with you here."

Her body swayed into his as they walked along the path. She peeked up at him, curiosity brimming in her eyes. "Is that so?"

"While you're here in Shady Springs, you'll have me to protect you. Me and my brothers don't take shit from no one."

She laughed, her brown eyes sparkling.

It was then Carson promised himself he'd do whatever he must to keep her smiling and laughing.

It was the most beautiful sound he'd ever heard.

Her smile brightened her face. He was captivated by her and was going to have to make sure they spent as much time as possible together before she left.

The bottom of his stomach gave way at the thought of her leaving.

They'd only just met.

Carson stared down in her chocolate-brown eyes and didn't want to think that.

7

Demi wasn't sure where Carson was leading her on the ranch. At the moment she didn't care if they just walked around in circles.

She'd follow him anywhere.

His personality was pulling her to him. He had her smiling and laughing immediately.

Even Hakim took to him easily in a short time span. It usually took her nephew a little to warm up to strangers, but one joke from Carson, and Hakim was grinning.

Demi was extremely protective of her nephew. His father wasn't in the picture, and Jaimie was a strong woman, raising her son on her own.

Demi refused to allow her sister to do it alone.

"So we are going to view the entire ranch on foot?" she asked. Demi had done research of her own on the Blazing Eagle and found it was a massive spread.

"Don't look like you wore your walking shoes." Carson's gaze dropped down to her feet.

Her sandals would not protect her feet from all of the dirt. She should have thought of better footwear before coming to the ranch.

"But that's all right. We're here."

They arrived to where some ATVs were parked in a row along the barn. Carson guided her over to one and assisted her in.

"These are nice," she said, settling in her seat.

"I'm sure it can't compare to Hollywood limos, but these babies get us around the ranch in no time." He jogged over to the driver's side and slid in.

"I don't ride in a limo every day." Demi rolled her eyes. She tilted her nose in the air playfully. "Only important affairs."

Carson barked a laugh and started the engine. He hit the gas, and they were off, heading down a dirt road.

Demi was amazed at the beauty of the open land. She missed this while living in LA. Just buildings, smog, and too many people.

Out here she could think.

She couldn't get enough of the wind blowing in her face, the scent of nature, and the sight of cows.

So many cattle.

She relaxed as Carson drove them around. It was a comfortable silence, allowing her to take in the sights.

"Tell me about yourself." She glanced at him.

He was the epitome of sexy cowboy. His strong forearm was stretched out while he maneuvered the steering wheel. His plaid shirt now covered a perfectly sculpted frame that she'd had the honor to see for about a minute before he'd thrown his shirt on.

When they had first arrived and Parker and introduced himself, he had been nice and taken them to where Carson was working.

When Carson had looked up from the tractor he had been working on, Demi had frozen in place.

Tan skin. A six-pack. Light sprinkling of hair and a few tattoos on his chest and one on his shoulder.

Demi had to force her tongue to work when he'd greeted her.

Carson appeared to be thinking of an answer for her. He tunneled a hand through his dark hair, pushing it away from his face.

"Well, let's see. I'm a Leo, the youngest of three boys, and I like to go on long walks in the country." He grinned, tossing a wink at her.

"I'm serious." She laughed and nudged him with her elbow.

"Okay, okay." He chuckled. "All of what I said before is true. I grew up here in Shady Springs, I went to college and graduated with a degree in business. Came back home and joined my family running this ranch."

Demi stared at him for a moment. For some odd reason, she wanted to know more.

"What about you, superstar?" he asked.

"Well, I grew up in Waco. I went to college, majored in music. I thought I was going to get my big break before I graduated. All little girls who grow up dreaming of becoming stars think it would happen overnight. I was one of them. It didn't happen. Left college and started working at a vocal school as a coach. I busted my butt any chance I could get to get into a studio. My first opportunity was landing an audition to be a backup singer."

Demi sat back, remembering the feeling she'd had when she heard she'd landed the job. She had been so ecstatic. It was as if she had won a million dollars. Deep in her heart, she knew it was the beginning for her. The gig wasn't for a superstar, but someone who was up-and-coming and touring across the country. It was the chance Demi needed to get her foot in the door. About two years later, she'd finally landed her big break.

And the rest, they say, is history.

"That's amazing," Carson said.

The vehicle slowed and turned down another path. The speed picked up slightly.

Demi glanced around and saw nothing but rolling acres before her. "It would seem that we are both able to do the things that we love."

Did she love what she did?

Singing? Of course.

Entertaining? Yes.

What she sang? She wouldn't say she was in love with it. Lately, it wasn't as fun for her. She loved the traveling, the concerts, but what she really wanted to do was sing what was in her heart.

"What's your favorite food?" she asked, changing the subject.

"A big ol' juicy steak. A loaded potato with all the works." He grinned at her.

Why had she even asked? He was a cattle rancher.

Of course steak would be in his top choice of food.

"What's your favorite movie?" Demi reached up and brushed her hair that was flying in the wind out of her face.

"I love the John Wick movies."

"Me, too," she exclaimed. She wasn't a chick flick movie fan. Demi preferred the kick-ass action movies that involved guns and buildings being blown to smithereens.

"I knew I liked you." Carson tossed her one of his panty-melting smiles. "You're over here asking me twenty questions. What's your favorite food?"

"Chocolate," she replied without hesitation.

"That's not a food." He laughed.

"It is," she replied superciliously. Demi had an unhealthy fascination with chocolate. She'd go crazy without it. "It goes well with a lot of things and it makes a lot of food better when it's covered in chocolate."

They fell into a comfortable silence again. It was amazing how much land the Brooks family owned. Demi lost track of time and didn't know how long they had been driving.

"How is a guy like you single?" Demi wasn't sure

where she got the courage to ask this, but apparently her brain wanted to know.

Carson shrugged. "I just figured I will let the universe decide for me. I'm sure I'll know her when I see her."

He glanced over at her, and Demi swallowed hard. The intense look sent butterflies to her stomach.

"What about you? Are you seeing someone?"

"Nope." She shook her head.

"How not? A beautiful gal like yourself? I'm sure you are beating the men away."

"I haven't really had the time for dating," she admitted.

"Damn, that doesn't seem fair in life."

Demi took in the scenery around them, finding a thick area of woods. It was breathtakingly gorgeous.

She would give anything to live in the country.

Her place in LA was nice, but it just wasn't her. No matter what she tried to do to it, she just couldn't seem to warm the place up. It didn't feel like a home.

He drove over to the trees and shut off the engine. He turned his gray eyes to her. Demi's heart skipped a beat.

"Come on, pretty lady." He hopped out of the vehicle and came around to help her out.

Their hands remained entwined. Demi wasn't going to stay a word. Carson's larger hand engulfed hers. It was warm, calloused, reminding her that he worked with his hands for a living.

She briefly wondered what those hands would feel like sliding along her thighs.

Demi blinked as a shiver commanded her body.

She had to try to keep her mind out of the gutter.

This was only their second day in each other's presence. She wasn't sure how he would respond to her thinking of them heating up the sheets together.

"Where are we going?" she asked.

"There's a creek right through these small woods that would be perfect for you to see." He guided them through the short thick of trees. The sounds of water running greeted them before the creek came into view.

"Oh my. This is beautiful," she breathed.

"Absolutely beautiful." Carson's hand tightened on hers.

She glanced over at him and found his gaze locked on her. Her face warmed slightly.

She didn't think he was speaking about the creek.

All of the feeling he was eliciting from her, had

her songwriting juices flowing. They moved over to a large tree and took a seat in front of it.

"What you see here is something that generations worked together to achieve," Carson murmured.

"Really?" She turned to him, interested in his family and the ranch. It intrigued her to learn about something that had been worked hard and passed down from one family member to the next.

"Yup, my great-great-grandfather moved to Shady Springs when it only had a feed store, a saloon, and a brothel where the town now stands."

"A brothel?" Demi chuckled. She had always been a person fascinated with history. She wasn't sure how people survived back then compared to the technology of today.

No planes. No cars. No cell phones.

Hell, no central air?

No, thank you.

"Oh, yeah. You know how they did it back in the eighteen-hundreds. They needed a little entertainment for the locals. All the farms stretched far and wide. The men needed something to occupy their time when not on the farms. They'd come into town to get a nice drink and the company of a woman." Carson winked at her.

"Is that so? And what do you do when you are not working on the ranch?" She raised a single eyebrow.

"Well, at the moment, I'm trying to catch the eye of a certain superstar, but not sure I'm in her league," he joked.

"Hey." She laughed, slapping his arm with the back of her hand.

"You asked, so I'll give you the truth." Carson shrugged. "Tell me about you, superstar."

Demi leaned back against the base of the tree. Her shoulder connected with Carson's arm. He didn't shy away from her.

"I grew up in Waco, Texas," she began. She was proud of her town. Any chance she got, she made sure her fans knew where she was from. When she made it big, she had put Waco on the map. "I have an elder brother, Frankie. He's the eldest of the three of us. Jaimie is the middle child, while I'm the baby."

"Ah, that explains so much," he murmured.

"Excuse me?" She turned to him, a smile on her lips. She constantly found her lips curved up with Carson. He just had a way about him that kept her entertained.

"Why we get along so well. You're the youngest, as am I."

"Hmm...you're right. We are both the youngest. You're probably spoiled," she said.

"Me?" He feigned surprise.

"Yeah, you. Who gets to grow up on the largest cattle ranch in the state, probably had whatever you wanted, and from the looks of you and your brothers, y'all probably stayed in trouble."

Carson barked a hefty laugh. Demi folded her arms in front of her, a giggle escaping her. He wiped his cheeks and shook his head.

"Okay, maybe I am. My brothers always had my back. Pops pretty much bought us whatever we wanted after my mother died. He didn't care. He just wanted us out of his hair and trouble, you just don't know the half of it."

His sexy grin had her stomach tied up in knots.

She knew it.

Carson had the face of someone who stayed in trouble. Demi could see clear through the innocent expression he was trying to keep on his face.

"Barroom fights and all, huh?"

He coughed playfully, wrapping an arm around her shoulders.

"Listen here, woman. I'm going to let you in on a secret. We Brooks men don't start fights, we are just damn good at ending them."

Demi rolled her eyes, groaning. "Can you be even cornier?"

They laughed, staring at each other. Demi was having a wonderful time with Carson. He was genuine, funny, and down to earth. They fell into a comfortable silence.

Demi stared off, loving the beauty of everything before them.

She was not missing the limelight at all. If only she could find a way to stay here forever. Just chilling out in the country without a care in the world.

"So tell me. When you look at the land, what do you see?" she asked quietly.

Carson pushed a hand through his hair, mussing the thick strands. He grew serious, turning his attention to the open range.

Since meeting him, she'd never seen him look this way.

"I see the future," he began. "My great-great-grandfather moved here, taking every dime he had to start something that has been passed on for generations. We were all taught about hard work at a young age. From the moment we could walk, our father had us working the land. He wanted to ensure that we took pride in what carries our name. One day I hope to pass my portion of the land down to my children and grandchildren."

"That's amazing," Demi breathed. She slid her arm through his and leaned her head on his shoulder.

"What do you see?" he asked, turning his curious gaze to her.

Demi inhaled sharply, taking in everything around them.

"Endless possibilities," she replied. Thoughts of her future came to mind. She respected how he and his family worked for what they loved. She loved performing and singing, but she wanted, she *needed* to do it her way.

That was why she was going to take back creative control of herself.

"What were you hoping to get from Shady Springs?" Carson asked.

She glanced down and wasn't certain when their fingers had become entwined. She tilted her head back so she could meet his gaze.

Demi was glad Carson had asked this question.

"One hell of a good time. I want to remember what it's like to just be a free, country girl with no worries."

A grin slowly spread across his face.

"You doing anything tomorrow night around eight?" he asked.

Demi shook her head.

"Well, superstar, I'll come pick you up at eight start. Put on your cowgirl boots, and a hat."

He kissed the back of her hand and helped her up. She stumbled slightly, her leg left a little numb from sitting in the same spot for so long. Her body melted against his. It was solid, the perfect representation of a hard-working rancher. Everywhere she was soft, he was muscle.

Something brushed against her stomach, and she held back a groan. Carson's eyes darkened, his hands resting on her waist. He closed the tiny gap between them.

"Okay. I think I packed them," she murmured.

"Good."

Carson gently pressed his lips to hers. Demi opened for him, inviting his tongue inside her mouth. He swept in, stroking her tongue. Demi slid her hands up the firm plain of his chest, locking them together at the base of his neck.

The kiss grew deeper, Carson angling his head to the side.

It was everything Demi could have hoped for in a first kiss.

Hot.

Heavy.

With plenty of tongue.

Her body warmed at the feeling of him pressed there. The image of him walking to her buttoning up his shirt would be forever ingrained in her memory.

But she wanted to see more.

From the feeling of his bulge, Carson Brooks was no small man.

Carson's hands found their way to her bottom, holding her in place. Not that she wanted to go anywhere. She was extremely content wrapped up in his embrace.

Something was vibrating on her. They broke apart, staring at each other.

Demi was blown away.

"I'm sure you need to get that," he murmured. His hand came up to her face, his finger running along her bottom lip.

She pulled her phone from her pocket. There was a text from her sister wondering where she was.

"Eight o'clock?" she asked, putting her phone back into her pocket. She only wanted a moment longer before having to go back to reality.

"Be ready to jump back into country life, superstar."

❦ 8 ❦

"This is a casual date," Demi murmured. She glanced at herself in the mirror and gave an appreciative nod to her reflection. According to Carson, she should wear something comfortable and bring out her boots and hat.

Well, if that was the case, she needed to dress the part.

She wore a pair of skinny jeans and a jean shirt that she tied up at the hems, leaving the top few buttons undone. She laughed, resembling a younger version of herself. Ambling over to her closet, she found her boots. These were casual, distressed leather, with studded detailing. It had been a while since she had worn them, but for some reason she had packed them for this trip.

She hopped around, pulling the boots on.

Slowly, Demi was feeling like herself again. For so long she had catered to who the music industry wanted her to be.

But inside, this was who she was.

Demi Day was a Texan who just wanted to be herself.

She walked into the attached master bathroom and chose one of her favorite perfumes and spritzed herself. She sat at the vanity and applied light makeup. Her hand shook slightly with her trying to imagine where Carson would be taking her.

She couldn't help but think of the last date she had been on. It had been a few months ago. She was back home in LA, collaborating with Kane Ace, one of the most popular rappers out.

Demi and Kane had known each other for a while. They had attended the same parties and had common friends.

She was invited to be featured on one of Kane's songs, and they had worked together in the studio. They had fun, and Kane had asked her out on a date.

Never again.

They were from two completely different backgrounds. He was from the hard streets of New York, while she was a country girl.

Demi cringed thinking of how the date had ended with him arguing with another rapper in a restaurant, a fire- and poop-throwing monkey.

They agreed to never speak of the date again.

Pushing down the memory of the date from hell, she thought of the man who would be arriving soon, and a smile came to her lips.

Carson Brooks.

Demi was barely able to get any work done today. The sexy cowboy with the crooked grin had stayed with her all day.

She was hiding from the world at the moment, but that didn't matter. The phones had been ringing off the hook with people wondering where she had disappeared to. She had shared she was going on a vacation without saying how long or the destination.

The world didn't need to know everything about her.

That was the downside of being a celebrity.

Everyone wanted to know everything about you.

Right now, Demi just wanted to be left alone.

There were too many things that needed her attention, and quite frankly, the only one she wanted to commit to worked on a ranch and wore the hell out of some Wrangler jeans.

Demi had finally answered the call from her

publicist. Rowan wasn't too happy she had left without a word but insisted she answer certain emails. He was trying to do his job, and a certain singer was keeping him from doing it.

It was common knowledge that Demi drove Rowan crazy.

But he was devoted to her and had calmed down once she'd ensured him she wasn't having a mental breakdown.

Rave, a popular music magazine, wanted an interview with her. They would come and meet her wherever she was and would photograph her also. They offered her the opportunity to be on the cover. She had responded that she would confer with her management team and forwarded it to Jaimie to schedule.

One call she couldn't refuse was that of her lawyer. She had spoken with Nina's and had set up a meeting with them.

Now that she had taken care of all her business obligations, she was ready to spend time with Carson.

Satisfied with her makeup and hair, she went back into her bedroom.

"Hey, Auntie." Hakim knocked on her door. He pushed it open slightly and peeked inside.

"Come on in." She motioned for him to enter.

He marched into the room and plopped down on her bed. He watched her pull her brown straw cowboy hat out of the closet.

"Where are you going?" he asked.

Demi placed the hat on her head and ruffled her fingers through her long tresses to straighten them out a bit. This was the first time she'd actually worn this hat. She had seen it in a store when she had gone home to Texas to visit. The craftsmanship gave it a unique stand-out appearance. It was rustic in nature, matching her boots.

"I have a date." She twirled around and grinned at him. She held out her hands and posed for him. "What do you think?"

"You're pretty as always." Hakim returned her smile. He pushed up on his elbow. "Are you going out with Tyler's uncle, Carson?"

"That I am." She spun around and walked over to the full-length mirror. She'd have to agree that she looked damn good.

"I had a lot of fun on the ranch, Auntie," Hakim said.

Demi made her way to the bed. She sat on the edge, attempting to grab his foot, but he was too quick. When he was younger, she'd learned he was extremely ticklish, and his feet were the worst.

"I'm glad you did. It was nice to see you smiling and having fun with someone your age."

"Do you think I could go back there?" He swiveled his big brown eyes to her.

Her heart leaped at the hope in his eyes. It didn't matter how much money she had, her poor nephew had been the target of bullies in school. Seeing him getting along with someone his age felt good.

"I don't see why not. I'm sure if we ask your mother, she will be okay with it."

"Learning about the animals was fun. Tyler took me around to see the other animals they keep on the land. Then his uncle's girlfriend came over and invited us over to her farm, too. She has sheep!"

Demi's heart melted at the look of excitement on his face. "Sheep? Really?"

"Yeah, a few of them followed her to the fence, and we got to pet them." Hakim sat up on the bed and swung his legs off the side.

"That sounds like fun. No wonder you want to go back."

"Tyler's nice. He's not like the other kids at school who used to pick on me." Hakim stood and took a few steps away. He faced her with a small smile on his face. "We want to hang out again, so I'm going to ask Mom if I can go back."

"What do you have planned for tonight?" she asked, following him out of the room.

"Um, video games." He snorted.

Demi rolled her eyes.

Of course.

Why did she even have to ask? Her nephew was addicted to his gaming system. A new version of a popular game had recently come out. He currently had straight A's in school, so his mother had purchased it for him.

"Well, have fun." She tousled his thick, short hair.

"You, too, Auntie." He jogged off toward his room.

Demi tuned her attention to finding her sister. She went downstairs in search of Jaimie. Demi found her sitting at the island in the kitchen, engrossed in whatever she was viewing on her laptop. A glass of wine stood next to her.

Jaimie looked up and grinned at her. "Well, who do we have here?"

Demi smiled, feeling silly. She circled around to model her outfit for her sister to see.

"Demi Day," Demi announced. "The real woman, not the singer."

"Can you really separate the two?" Jaimie asked, her smile fading.

They both knew the answer.

No, she couldn't. As much as she tried to, no matter where she went, she was always *the* Demi Day.

But here in Shady Springs, she was able to be herself.

"Today, I'm just me. Your little sister." She moved over to Jaimie who enveloped her in her arms. They shared a tight hug before Demi pulled away.

"I know you don't want to hear this, but I went through your emails that you forwarded me and was going to schedule the *Rave* photo shoot and interview. Are you sure you want to do it here?"

"I do. With what we are planning, I think it will be perfect." Demi leaned against the counter. "I think this can be something different than the edgy shoots I normally do. This will be more me. Fresh air, country backdrop..." Demi let her voice trail off.

Jaimie's eyes lit up. "Oh, I see what you are doing," she murmured. She tapped out a few more commands on her computer, bringing up Demi's calendar. "Next week, we have a meeting with the lawyers. They are all coming here. I'll check the availability of *Rave*."

"Here? Why?" Demi was confused. Why would the entire team need to meet here in Shady Springs? What was so important that the suits had to come to her home?

"Because I just got confirmation that Nina will be here. She wants to meet with you personally about all of this and she told the lawyers to get their butts here."

"Okay." Demi was really impressed by how many people jumped when Nina wanted something done.

"And, we have a virtual meeting with the representatives from Adore Me the following week."

Demi blew out a deep breath. She glanced at Jaimie's glass of wine, but her sister must have guessed her intention and picked it up.

"Don't even think of touching my glass." Jaimie scoffed. "With as much work I have to do, I'll be finishing off this bottle tonight."

"You love me, though." Demi grinned.

"I do and I know how much you need a nice night on the town without all the cameras and paparazzi. When is he picking you up?" Jaimie asked.

Demi glanced down at her watch. Her heart skipped a beat. It was almost time.

"He said eight." She shrugged nonchalantly.

"Well, go have enough fun for the both of us. I'll be sitting here going through the rest of your emails and setting up meetings and doing my job."

"I'll throw in a bonus for you." Demi chuckled, backing away.

"I did see that new Broncho truck they just brought out," Jaimie said.

"It's yours, pick it out." Demi winked. She loved that she could spoil her family. Hard work had paid off, and she could afford whatever she wanted in life. She spun around to go find her purse when the doorbell sounded.

It would appear Mr. Brooks was a timely man.

Demi rushed to the front door. From the foyer, she could see his tall frame standing outside through the double glass doors. She opened the door and almost forgot how to breathe.

Carson turned to her, leveling his dark gaze on her.

They stood staring at each other for a moment.

Her gaze roamed his form, finding him in a long-sleeved dark shirt, jeans, and boots.

"Well, howdy." His deep baritone voice sent a tremor down Demi's spine.

"Hi." She cleared her throat, frozen in place. How

the hell did this man look so damn good? The shirt may have covered his entire chest and torso, but she could still make out the hard plains of his body through it. "Please come in." She waved him in, shutting the door behind him.

"Nice place. I haven't been here since before they renovated it and put it up on that rental website," Carson said, glancing around.

"You know the owners?" She walked over to him.

"Yeah, the widow moved from Shady Springs once her husband died. She went to stay with her kids, but they wanted to keep the house. They usually come back in the wintertime for skiing and vacations."

His cologne reached her senses, and she just wanted to step over to him and bury her face into his shirt. She wanted to breathe him in.

The memory of their kiss to came to mind.

"Let me grab my purse." She spun around, searching for it. She found it on the couch in the living room. Snatching it up, she yelled out to her sister, "I'm gone!"

"Have fun!" Jaimie hollered from the kitchen.

Demi returned to Carson, finding him in the same spot. A smile spread across his face.

"Ready now?" he asked.

"Yes, sir." She'd laid on her Texan accent thick.

He held out his hand for her. She immediately slid hers into it and allowed him to guide her out of the house.

Demi was dying to know where they were going.

He chuckled, entwining their fingers. He led them over to his pickup truck and assisted her into the vehicle.

The scent of him was even stronger in the cab. She inhaled sharply, making a note to ask him what cologne he had on. There was nothing sexier than a man who took the time to make sure he smelled good.

Carson shut the door, jogging over to the driver's side, and got in. His sexy grin was still in place as he glanced over at her.

"All right, superstar. I hope you are ready for a night of good ol' country fun." He tossed a wink her way and put the truck in drive.

Carson couldn't breathe. He was laughing so hard. He sat at the table in the bar he'd brought Demi to and couldn't stop laughing.

She was out on the dance floor, line dancing with all the locals. He'd had a feeling coming to the Rusty Spur was going to be perfect.

Food, line dancing, and karaoke.

Country style.

Demi's grin was from ear to ear as she turned and moved along with the crowd. She blended in with the locals, and her hat and sexy boots had her looking like she'd been in Colorado all her life.

"Want a refill?" The server stopped by the table and motioned to their glasses.

She offered a wide smile, but Carson had eyes for only one woman.

"Please." He nodded before rotating around to watch Demi have her fun. Brooks men did not dance.

Ever.

Even though Maddy had been known to make Parker.

Not Carson.

He was good at a lot of things and knew his limit. Dancing was not one of them. The good Lord above had blessed him with two left feet.

He was very content with watching Demi burn up the floor. Her curves were on display by her outfit, and he couldn't take his eyes off her.

She had been noticed from the moment they had stepped foot in the bar. The older people didn't know who she was, but the younger ones certainly did.

Demi had posed with fans for pictures and greeted them all. They'd all gushed over her just as Maddy had done.

There were even some women with their phones up, recording Demi. Carson glanced around, not sensing any threat. He'd remembered joking about security and her admitting she did have bodyguards who were a phone call away.

He didn't like the fact that she would need to

have a security detail, but at least she was safe. Shady Springs was as safe as a town could be.

"Oh my. I haven't line danced in ages." Demi giggled, arriving at his side.

He roped an arm around her and brought her to stand between his legs. The chairs at the table were high-up stools, and it allowed her to rest back along his chest.

"You look like you were having fun," he remarked.

She spun around in his arms, the excitement evident on her face.

"I am. Thank you so much for this. I really needed it." Her smile slowly faded.

Carson reached up and slid a finger along her cheek. Her soft brown skin called to him.

She leaned into him, wrapping her arms around his waist. She tilted her head back, her lips parting slightly.

He read the message loud and clear.

He bent down, touching his lips to hers in a soft, gentle kiss. Her taste was sweet, and Carson wanted more of her.

He pulled back slightly, not wanting to get carried away in a public place.

"Glad you are enjoying yourself." Carson smiled.

He found himself wanting to always be the reason she smiled. He motioned to the table. "Want to order anything else to eat?"

They had only ordered appetizers to get them started, but then the music had begun, and the folks made their way out to the dance floor. Demi had been out there for almost every song.

"I am famished. Dancing always works up my appetite." She chuckled.

"What do you have a taste for?"

She spun around in his arms and lifted the small menu that had been left on the table. They were in no rush to leave. Carson was having fun, and he wanted to spend more time with Demi.

He wanted to get to know her. There was an attraction to her that he couldn't explain.

The fact that she wasn't in Shady Springs to stay got pushed to the back of his mind.

He looked over her shoulder while she studied the menu.

"Most of this will go straight to my hips," she muttered.

"I'm not complaining at all." Carson chuckled. He ran his hand along her hip appreciatively. He preferred his woman to have plenty of feminine curves.

"Of course you can say that." She grinned. She turned and pinched his side. "You have no fat whatsoever. How is that?"

Carson patted his stomach with a shrug. "It's called hard labor on a ranch from sunup to sundown, seven days a week for most of my life." He tugged her close and dropped a kiss on her cheek. "I'd be interested in showing you some other type of exercises that help burn fat."

Demi chewed on her lip, and Carson bit back a groan. It was a little sexy move she did unconsciously. He wanted to move her teeth and nibble on her lip himself.

"Hmmm…is that so?" Her perfectly sculpted eyebrows rose. "And you are certified in this type of exercise program?"

Carson's grin spread wider.

"Superstar, you're going to be the judge of that." He winked at her.

She looked away, but it wasn't before he saw the heat flare in her eyes.

His little songstress was just as interested in him as he was in her.

The server returned. "Here's your drinks." She sat their two beers down on the table and stood watching them with a friendly smile on her face.

"Can I get you something else to eat or were you good with the appetizers?"

"Rose, I think I'm going to order the bacon cheeseburger with fries," Demi announced.

Rose pulled out her pad and pen and wrote down Demi's order.

"I'll have the same. Make mine a double cheeseburger," Carson said. He was famished. He had a huge appetite and never worried about things such as gaining weight.

Rose scribbled, finishing taking their order, then she disappeared. Demi pulled her stool close and got up on it. Carson instantly missed having her so near to him.

"I hope you are not seriously worried about your weight?" he asked, eyeing Demi. She was perfect in his eyes.

"Not really. I have a trainer when I'm back in California, who I swear is a sadist and takes great pleasure in my pain." She grimaced and reached for her beer.

The crowd in the bar was getting thicker. The country music blared through the speakers. Everyone was having a good time. Some patrons glanced over at Demi curiously but kept their distance.

"Do you like living in California?" He sensed there was something she wasn't saying. Whenever she spoke of where she lived, a weird expression briefly came across her face then disappeared.

"It's convenient for work, but not really. There's too many people. I prefer wide-open spaces." She glanced down at her hands, biting her lip again.

He reached for it and took her small hand in his. He rubbed the back of it with his thumb.

"Why don't you move? You can live anywhere, right? Do you have to be in California?"

"No. I don't have to. There's a lot on my mind now. Big decisions that are going be life-altering that I have to make in the coming weeks."

"Sounds tough." The only major decision he had made in his life was which school he was going to sign on to play football. He'd known he didn't want to go professional, the ranch was always his destiny. "Well, if you need an ear to listen, I'm here for you, Demi."

Her gaze flicked to his. She stared at him for a moment. She squeezed his hand, a ghost of a smile reappearing on her lips.

"Thanks, Carson. I really appreciate it."

He brought her hand to his lips and kissed the back of it.

If she were here to escape her problems and demands of her career, then he was going to make sure she enjoyed herself and had plenty of distractions.

"It's karaoke hour!" a deep voice announced over the speaker system.

The crowd cheered, excitement growing through the place. Karaoke night at the bar was one of the popular events in town.

"Oh my!" Demi twisted around to look back at dance floor that was now filled with people standing around waiting for the first brave person to get up on the little stage.

It was always one or two people who'd get up there and could carry a note. Most couldn't sing, but it wasn't about that. It was all about having fun.

Add in alcohol, and everyone had a grand ol' time.

"You have to go up there." Carson chuckled. He saw the yearning in her eyes.

She spun around and grinned. "You think?"

"Hell yeah. Get up there and sing a little country. Show us how y'all Texans do it."

DEMI'S PULSE POUNDED. IT WASN'T THAT she was afraid to get up and sing in front of a crowded bar. She'd sung in front of tens of thousands and didn't break a sweat.

This was for fun.

She didn't care what anyone thought in here, except one person.

Those gray eyes were on her, and they rattled her.

The kisses, light touches, and the offer of a certain exercise that helped burn fat had her strung tight.

She wanted Carson.

There was no question about it.

Her stomach was in knots.

Would he make the move tonight? If he invited her back to his place, would she go?

Hell. Yeah.

In a heartbeat. Hell, she'd drive them to his house to get him naked and thrusting inside her.

She'd felt him pressed up against her and she knew he was a large man, but what was vying for her attention was definitely massive.

Demi had signed her name on the wait list for a turn to sing. The man before her was currently singing. Horribly, but the crowd was loving it.

Apparently, karaoke was popular in Shady Springs.

People were packed like sardines on the former dance floor.

She navigated her way through the people to go stand by the stairs to the tiny stage. It was probably the smallest one she had ever performed on, but it would do. Sometimes it wasn't about the stage or the amount of people.

It was their reactions and enjoyment that Demi thrived off of.

When she'd first begun performing, it was in little establishments like this.

Thanks to social media, she'd taken off and was able to get noticed.

Demi hadn't been sure anyone would recognize her in the bar. She was taken by surprise by the amount of townsfolk who knew who she was. They were all friendly and in awe that she was in their remote town. She'd taken photos with them and was sure by morning, it would be all over the media where she was.

Her cell phone had been buzzing like crazy, but she'd ignored it. At the moment, all that mattered was having fun with her cowboy.

Demi stood by the stairs and pulled her hat down

farther on her head. When did Carson become her cowboy?

That first kiss.

Little did he know, he was hers.

Without a doubt, something was shared between the two of them. There was a strong connection. Demi had sung enough about love songs to realize that she knew she couldn't pass up on what was brewing.

How they'd make it work, she'd have to figure it out.

There were plenty of professional performers who married someone not in the business.

Marry?

"Slow down, girl." Demi giggled.

Did she want a long-term commitment? A husband? Kids?

Without a doubt she did.

She looked over to where Carson sat and found him staring at her. He lifted his beer to her.

She blew him a kiss. He smiled, acting as if he caught it.

He could be corny, sweet, and sexy.

The perfect combination.

The crowd cheering broke through her thoughts.

She turned back to see the gentleman exiting the stage from the other end.

"Up next, we have a newcomer to Shady Springs. Demi Day!" The announcer's deep baritone voice was drowned out by the women screaming.

Every bit of nervousness vanished the second she stalked up the stairs to the mini stage.

Demi grinned, waving to them. Flashes went off. The sea of cameras let her know she would definitely be all over the internet. It was amazing how quick something could spread.

The coordinator handed her a mic, and she was in her comfort zone.

Demi had held a mic in her hand since she was ten years old. This was something she was born to do.

"How y'all doing?" Demi let her Texan roots show. There was no one to tell her to pull back on her accent.

Tonight, she was just Demi.

Country at heart.

Seeing the gazes of people in awe brought her right back to her start. She was humbled that this crowd, not her usual, was excited to hear what she was bringing tonight.

"I love you, Demi!" someone shouted.

"Oh, I love you, too." Demi faced the direction of the fan and winked. "Now I know some of you may not know me, and that's all right. We're all having a good time tonight! Is that right?"

"Yeah!" the crowd roared.

All eyes in the bar were on her. The lights blared, keeping her from seeing Carson, but she could feel his gaze on her.

"That's what I want to hear! But tonight, this is for the ladies. Where are my sexy women?"

The women screamed, holding up their drinks and phones, pushing toward the stage. Demi grinned, motioning for the guy who was in charge of the music. She had the perfect song she'd been dying to cover. It was one of her favorite songs by Shania Twain. What better place to do it than now? The beat began, and the place went berserk.

"Let's go, girls. Come on!"

Demi danced around, adrenaline rushing through her. She brought the mic to her lips and the words flowed.

Just as she thought. It was perfect. Every woman in the building was singing right along with her. She held the mic out so they could sing the pre-chorus.

Demi laughed, the women drunkenly singing word for word and not missing a beat. For them, this song must be ingrained in them just as it was for Demi.

Demi remembered when it was first released. She must have played it over a million times to where her CD started skipping.

Demi brought the mic back to her, coming to her favorite part.

"Oh-oh-oh, go totally crazy!"

Demi couldn't remember the last time she'd had so much fun performing.

This solidified what she should do.

Now there was no doubt in her mind. She was going to follow her dreams.

Carson led Demi from the bar by the hand. He had been unable to keep his hands from her. He was still in awe of her singing.

Her voice was like none he'd ever heard. Maddy had played her music around the house, but he had to stay that she sounded better live.

The crowd didn't let her get away with one song.

Demi sung four before coming off the stage. Each one had the audience singing and dancing right along with her.

The atmosphere in the bar had been electric. Everyone was captivated by her voice, her smile, and personality.

He was sure she would be the talk of the town by morning.

"Demi!" someone shouted.

She turned and gave them a wave as they continued walking to his truck. Laughter filled the air from the patrons who were lingering around in the parking lot.

Carson had to admit he was the luckiest guy in the world. From the moment she had stepped off the stage, Demi's full attention had been on him. He'd seen the looks from the men in the bar, all giving her an appreciative eye. There were a few that Carson had to give a threatening look to get them to stop staring at his girl.

Demi stayed close; her touches, kisses, were driving him crazy. She found every open opportunity to stand between his legs when he was sitting, kissing his chin or neck.

Her curvy frame fit against his perfectly.

He was fighting the urge to adjust himself. His cock was straining against his jeans.

"Everyone is just so nice." Demi laughed.

"They are in love with you." He wrapped an arm around her shoulders, yanking her closer to him. "Woman, you have an amazing voice."

They arrived at the passenger side of his truck. Demi smiled, tilting her head back to meet his gaze.

"Really? Is that all you noticed tonight?" She dusted an invisible piece of lint off his shirt.

He growled playfully, trapping her between him and the door. He rested his hands on each side of her head, trapping her with his body.

"There's plenty that I noticed." He ground his pelvis against her to show her how much she was affecting him.

Demi's hands skated up his chest and entwined at the base of his neck. He lowered his head and met her lips in a sizzling kiss.

Demi opened for him, allowing his tongue to slide into her mouth. He stroked her tongue with his, unable to get enough of her taste.

Demi's moan was swallowed by the kiss. Her body pressed closer to his while the kiss deepened. Her fingers dove into his hair, sending a tremor down his spine.

He needed her.

A car horn blared, snapping him back to reality. Carson lifted his head, remembering where they were.

"My place?" He attempted catch his breath.

"God, yes," she gasped.

He hurriedly ushered her into the truck before jogging over to his side. He slid in, starting the engine. The wheels tore up the rocks and dirt in the parking lot as he peeled out. He guided them onto the road and pushed the speed limit.

"Thank you," Demi said quietly.

"For what?" he asked, trying to concentrate on the road.

"Being you. Taking me out for fun and not wanting anything for it."

He glanced at her and felt a small twinge of pity for her.

Did people use her because of her fame?

"I'm not that type of person, Demi. Besides, I have almost everything a man could want in life." He took her hand and kissed it. She was going to have to learn what it meant to be treated as an equal and loved by a Brooks man. "It was fun watching you have the time of your life."

Love?

They hadn't known each other long, but he was growing to care for her. He didn't think they were at the love stage yet.

But he did care for her.

She shifted in her seat, drawing his attention back to her. He just about swallowed his tongue. She'd opened her shirt completely, revealing her sexy bra. He took in the swell of her breasts through the sheer dark material.

"Demi," he rasped. His mouth was suddenly dry, his tongue sticking to the roof of his mouth. "What are you doing?"

She gave him one of her seductive smiles and took her shirt off completely, throwing it in the back of the cab.

"Well, I know you want me just as much as I want you. I figured I'd go ahead and get one thing out of the way." She laughed. She reached over and combed her fingers through his hair.

"You are crazy." He chuckled, shaking his head.

"How much longer until we get to your house?" she asked, her eyebrows arched high.

"Ten minutes." He turned his gaze to the road, trying to concentrate. Thank goodness, this bar wasn't too far from the ranch. His cock pressed hard against his jeans. Carson's pulse pounded in his ears. He glanced back at Demi who had taken her boots off and was currently shimming out of her jeans. "Fuck. Five minutes."

He pressed his foot down on the gas. At this time of night, the sheriff's department were probably too busy with patrolling the bar scene to care about someone speeding down an empty highway road.

Demi giggled, reaching over, and pulled something down over his head. His gaze flickered to what rested around his neck.

Her panties.

Shit.

"You better hurry, Carson," her voice was low and husky.

The sound of it sent a bolt of lightning straight to his dick.

"I might get this party started without you."

"Like hell you are."

Fuck, her bra was gone.

The sexiest woman in the world was currently naked in his passenger seat, running her hands along her full breasts.

He flicked his gaze between Demi and the road.

"Where do you think those hands of yours are going?" he growled.

She laughed, her hand edging toward her thighs.

He reached over and captured her hand in his. "Oh, no. That's for me tonight."

"I know." She took control of his hand and led it in between her soft thighs.

With his eyes on the road, he parted her labia with his finger, finding her soaked.

A curse escaped him.

The turn to the ranch was coming up.

"Just hold on a second," he murmured. He slowed the pickup, taking the turn. He sped down the dirt road. He knew the layout of the land like the back of his hand.

"Carson…" Her throaty moan filled the cab. He slid his finger onto her slick nub and just about came undone.

They weren't going to make it into the house.

His cock was painfully hard, and all Carson could think about was sinking inside her slick channel.

Demi's gasp met his ear as he stroked her clit. It was swollen, engorged, and waiting for him. He drove to his house in record time. Thankfully, he and his brother's houses were on different sectors of the family land.

He parked the truck at the back of his house near the detached garage, killing the engine.

"You are going to be the death of me," he murmured. Slipping his finger from between Demi's thighs, he brought it up to his lips to get his first taste of her.

Her taste exploded on his tongue. A growl escaped him.

He wanted more.

"Oh shit," she whispered, her eyes locked on him.

"Hold that thought, Demi." He exited the truck and snatched open the back door. He pulled out the blanket he kept there and slammed the door shut.

He opened the hitch to the bed of the truck and spread the blanket down. The moon was high and centered in the dark sky.

Carson made his way to the passenger door and opened it.

"Come here," he murmured.

Demi wrapped her arms and legs round him. The heat of her core met his stomach. He could feel it radiating from her through his shirt.

She slammed her mouth on his, thrusting her tongue inside his mouth. Her tongue stroked his, coaxing his to come inside her mouth.

Her hands dove into his hair, and the kiss deepened. He made it to the back of the truck and lay her down on the blanket.

The last time he'd had a girl in the back of his pickup was high school.

But this was different.

There was no way in hell they were going to make it into the house. There was an urgent need for his cock to enter Demi's soaked channel.

"Carson, hurry," she gasped, tugging his shirt from his jeans.

Carson undid the first few buttons before pulling it over his head. He kicked off his boots while her hands fell to the belt buckle and button of his jeans.

"Shit, girl." He chuckled, his hands trembling as he unzipped his jeans. He pushed them and his boxer briefs down. His thickened shaft sprang out, and he kicked himself free of his clothes.

Demi's legs widened to allow him to settle between the valley of her thighs.

He covered her mouth with his.

He wanted to taste every part of her.

Damn that they were outside in the back of his truck like two horny teenagers.

There was nothing like making love under the open sky and full moon.

Demi's nails raked along his back. He thought it sexy for a woman to know what she wanted and going after it.

Carson buried his face in the crook of her neck. He breathed in her scent, traveling down to her breasts. He bathed both of her perky nipples with his tongue. Next time, they would be in his bed, and he wanted to see every single inch of her.

For now, feeling her would have to do. He slid his hands along her mounds, testing their weight. They fit his hands perfectly.

"Carson," she moaned.

"Tell me, baby. What do you want?"

"You. I need you inside me now," she cried out.

Carson chuckled, slowly moving down her body. He ran his tongue along her belly, tasting her, and continued his travels south.

He pushed her legs open wider so he could take her all in. The scent of her arousal greeted him. Carson licked his lips, ready to devour the woman before him.

He pecked kisses to her inner thighs, torturing her. Her curses and incomprehensible words floated through the air.

He chuckled. Her fingers snagged his hair and tried to direct him to her center.

"I got this." He snickered.

"Are you sure?" She laughed.

He spread her labia open and dove in. His tongue

dipped into her core then arrived at her clit. Her hips arched up to meet him.

"Ahh…" Her moan echoed through the air.

He captured her clit and teased her, flicking it with his tongue, suckling it into his mouth.

There was no need to rush.

He had all night.

Demi writhed beneath him.

He pushed a finger into her. Her slick walls surrounded him, and he thrust it in and out of her. He latched on to her nub, applying sweet pressure to the bundle of nerves.

"Carson," she chanted repeatedly.

He introduced another finger, stretching her to prepare her for him. He pumped them in and out of her while paying close attention to her nub.

Demi's muscles tensed, her legs closing in around his head. Carson laughed, pushing her legs apart to keep her from smashing his head.

She came undone.

Her low moan vibrated through her, growing into a scream of ecstasy. Her body trembled beneath his touch.

Carson's pulse pounded in his ears. He gave her one last lick, officially addicted to her taste. He kissed her inner thigh, climbing over her and bracing himself so he could watch her.

Demi laid beneath him with her eyes closed. The bright moon allowed him to see the thin film of sweat coating her body. Her lips were curled up into a small smile.

She opened her eyes and returned his gaze. He cocked an eyebrow and stared up at her.

"What?" she asked.

"Well, you didn't seem to trust that I knew what I was doing," he teased.

"Seriously, you are looking for compliments?"

He grinned and shrugged. His cock hung low, brushing against her soaked slit. He lowered himself down on her, resting most of his weight on his forearms.

"Not yet." He kissed her swollen lips. "Once I'm done with you, I will expect a full review of my performance."

Demi barked a laugh that soon died the second he lined the blunt tip of his cock at her entrance. He slowly pushed forward, locking eyes with her.

The air was snatched from his lungs at the sensation of her slippery channel accepting him. Demi raised her leg up high on his waist as he sank into her.

"Demi," he moaned, tucking his face into the crook of her neck.

He was fully seated. His hips remained still through fear of the party ending soon.

"Carson," she gasped.

Her core clenched, and he shuddered.

He withdrew slightly, leaving just the tip inside her, then thrusting forward again. Her breathless gasp fueled his desire for her.

He needed to claim her.

He set a steady rhythm that she matched. She held on, digging her nails into his shoulders.

Their gasps and moans filled the air. The coolness of the wind blew, but Carson barely felt it. His body was overheating.

Sweat slid down the plains of his back. Their bodies molded together.

Demi was made for him.

Carson lifted his head and crushed his lips to hers. Demi's lips parted, allowing his tongue to slip inside. He stroked her tongue with his.

He pushed harder.

Her nails dug deeper.

An electrical current traveled through his body. The truck rocked with the force of their movement.

Carson slid a hand down her torso and between

them. His finger arrived at her tiny bud, swollen, peeking from between her labia.

He strummed it gently with his thumb, wanting her to explode around him.

"Carson."

The sound of his name on her lips drove that fire inside him. Knowing it was him who was bringing her this type of pleasure did something to him. He didn't know what, but he loved that she was calling his name. Her scratching his back motivated him.

"I need you to come again, baby," he murmured, his lips brushing hers. He was always a giving lover, and giving her multiple orgasms was his main goal.

Would always be.

Carson wanted to be the only one who brought her to climax.

"I'm almost there," she gasped. Her arms tightened around him, tugging him to her, allowing her to bury her face against his shoulder. Her teeth scraped along his neck.

Her body shook beneath him. Her grip on him grew tight while she threw her head back with another cry of ecstasy.

Carson could no longer hold back. Demi's core contracted on him, and he roared with his release.

His lungs burned with the need to draw in

breath. He collapsed on top of her, unable to move. Demi cradled him to her, both of their bodies coated with sweat.

Carson was finally able to drag air into his lungs. He pushed up, not wanting to crush her. He rolled over to his side, his cock slipping from her warm sheath. He pulled her to him, not wanting to ever let her go.

❧ 11 ❧

"**N**o snoring," Carson's voice broke through the fog that consumed Demi.

She turned, resting her face against his chest.

"What you hiding for now?" His laughter filled the air.

She knew she'd had a few drinks at the bar, but she hadn't been sloppy drunk. Maybe a little tipsy, and that was probably why she had tossed all inhibitions to the side.

The entire time at the bar, she'd just felt a connection with Carson that she couldn't explain. He was everything she would ever want in a man.

Sexy with a sense of humor and confident in who

he was. He didn't have to compete for the limelight. He was successful in what he did and enjoyed life.

He'd kept a smile on her face the entire time they were together. Once they walked out to the car, she'd known she wanted to take their relationship to the next level.

Yes, she knew it had only been a few days, but she knew what she wanted.

What Demi wanted, she would get.

Stripping in the truck hadn't been the plan, but once she'd started she couldn't help herself. The scorching look in his eyes had fueled the fire for him.

Her body had ached in a way it had never done before, and it was all because of Carson.

"I can't believe I did that," she replied, her voice muffled by his bare chest.

When they were finally able to move, Carson had helped her put on his shirt to cover her up. The cool night air gave her goosebumps.

She turned her head and rested it on his shoulder, staring up at the sky. It had been a long time since she was able to just do what she wanted without having to worry about what someone at the record label would say.

"Did what?" Carson's hand lazily trailed along

her back. They were wrapped up in the blanket, gazing at the stars.

"Acted the way I did in the car. That is so not me," she admitted sheepishly.

"I thought the person in the truck with me who decided to strip off her clothes was downright sexy." Carson kiss her forehead.

Demi groaned in embarrassment. Who was that hussy back there?

"There is nothing sexier than a woman taking the initiative to tell a man she wants him," he said.

"What if you would have gotten pulled over by the police?" She gasped. That would have been the last thing she needed to hit the media. Rowan would kill her for the nightmare he would have to clean up.

His chest vibrated from the deep chuckle.

"Believe me, it wouldn't have been the first time I had to wiggle my way out of trouble with the cops." Carson laughed. "I'm on first-name basis with practically the entire sheriff's department."

"What? Carson Brooks has run-ins with the law?" she drawled.

"More times than you should know." He grimaced.

"Seriously? When was the last time you were arrested?" Demi wanted to learn everything she could about her cowboy. Apparently, he had a bad-born streak she needed to find out about.

"Me and my brothers went out to the country music fair not too long ago. Parker had brought Maddy along, but me and Wade had been hanging out at the bar. Had some drinks to help drown out his sorrows because he and Joy had broken up. Joy's brother showed up and picked a fight. My brothers and I ended it."

"With the police carting you off to jail?" She rested her chin on her hand that lay on his chest, studying him. Everything he was saying was giving her an idea. It was amazing how inspiring Shady Springs had been for her. Words were just floating around in her head.

Nothing like writing a song about a cowboy who was a bad boy.

She slid back down and snuggled into his side.

"Yeah." Carson's grin faded as he stared into the dark sky. The moon was still high with little twinkles of the stars that littered the black backdrop.

They fell into a comfortable silence.

Demi allowed her hand to trace along Carson's chest. He had a light sprinkling of hair that trailed down toward his shorts. Carson's hand came to rest on top of hers.

"You are going to get things started if you go any lower," he murmured.

His lips brushed her forehead. Demi's body was responding to his. She wasn't sure when she had ever wanted someone as much as she wanted Carson right now.

"Well, you did say that you liked a woman who went after what she wanted." She smirked.

"Did I say that?"

"Something close enough." She grinned. Her hand broke free of his grip and landed on his bulge. His cock was stiff underneath her touch. To tease him more, she cupped him, squeezing gently. "And if you haven't picked up on it, I want more of this."

She dropped a kiss on his chest. The scent of him assaulted her senses. He smelled of sandalwood, a light musk, and the outdoors.

Everything a man should smell like.

"Well, then, pretty lady. I say we head into my house and continue this party on my nice comfortable king-sized bed." He grimaced.

His back must be taking the brunt of them lying on the bed of his truck. She had been all over him the second he'd opened the door of the vehicle. She didn't know where that had come from, but the result had been fabulous.

"Lead the way." She sat up, combing her hair with her fingers. She was sure she looked a hot mess. Her clothes were still inside the truck along with her purse and phone.

Carson slid from the bed and turned to reach for her. He lifted her down, holding her in his arms.

"I can walk, you know." For some reason her arms were finding themselves wrapped around his neck.

"Yes, but I just want to keep you in my arms."

Demi's heart melted.

What was she going to do when it came time for her to leave Shady Springs?

"So you performing in small town bars now?" Rowan's voice came down the line.

Demi rolled her eyes. She knew that it was going to make all of the social media outlets. Her face and performance at the bar were splashed everywhere. Her phone had been ringing off the hook from the moment she'd returned home from Carson's house.

"Rowan, don't be mad. It was me out with a friend and having fun," she murmured. She tucked her towel around her body and sat on the bed. She had just finished her shower when her phone rang. She had pretty much ignored it for the last twenty-four hours.

Now she knew she'd better answer the phone when Rowan was calling.

"And singing country? I thought the label said they wanted you to stick to R&B?"

"Well, I may not have to worry about that," she replied frankly.

His gasp echoed through the phone.

"Are you really going to go through with it? Rumor had it that you've been thinking of not re-signing. Have you found another label?"

"Rowan, you should know better than to listen to gossip," she said. "Not everything you hear is true, and you should also know that I will tell you what I'm doing the minute I know."

"I know, but a lot of people have been wanting to know. I need to put something out there to settle everyone."

Demi rolled her eyes again. The media was like vultures. They wanted to sink their teeth into a good story and tell all of her business.

Rowan was a sweetheart, but he loved to gossip.

He was very good at his job, and that's why she paid the money she did to make sure he was happy.

"Why don't I fly you out here where you can join me. Fresh air will do you some good."

"Oh no. You know me and country life don't mix well. I need to have my smog, expensive coffees, and all the boogieness that LA can offer."

Demi snorted. She knew Rowan was a man who loved the city and wouldn't be caught dead in a rural area.

"You are such a diva," she muttered.

"And what is this I hear that you have found a new beau?" His voice dropped low.

She could tell he had his gossip hat on. She trusted him and knew he wouldn't spill the 'tea' as he would say. He just thrived on hearing gossip.

"Well, I may have met someone," she began.

His squeal had a grin spreading across her face. Demi stood and went over to her closet. Today was Parker and Maddy's wedding day. She was honored to attend a fan's wedding.

Demi entered the small walk-in closet and headed straight toward the outfit she had purchased for today. It was a lilac off-the-shoulder dress that brushed her knees. She had the perfect sandals that would be comfortable, and it just so happened she had the perfect oversized floppy straw hat.

"From the grainy photos I saw, he looks like a tall drink of water." Rowan chuckled.

"He's amazing." She sighed. Thoughts of their night together floated to her mind. He hadn't taken her home until a little after six in the morning. He was late getting to work, but he'd had a very good excuse. "I'm having fun here. It's good to meet someone who is enjoying me for me, and not what I can do for him."

"That's sweet, babe. Well, you go have fun with your cowboy. I heard about the meeting from Jaimie, you just let me know what you want put out and I'll take care of everything."

Demi was comforted by his offer. With her hiding away in Shady Springs, Rowan had been fielding many inquiries about her.

"Thanks. I got to go."

They disconnected the call. Demi took the dress and strolled back to the bed to lay it across the mattress.

She tossed her phone on the nightstand. Carson had planned to pick her up a little early so he could help out with last-minute things for the wedding.

She had offered to just drive to the ranch, but he'd insisted on picking her up.

She ambled into the bathroom and put on light makeup and fixed her hair. She flat ironed it to fall in waves around her shoulders. For some reason, Colorado was having a warm start to fall, and the material would keep her cool while the hat would keep the sun out of her eyes.

Satisfied with her appearance, she went back into her bedroom so she could finally get dressed. A knock sounded at the door. It was probably Jaimie coming to be nosey.

"Come in," she called out, moving over to her dresser. She hadn't picked out her undies yet, and she needed to do that quickly before Carson showed up.

"Looks like I came just in time," a deep baritone voice said from the doorway.

Demi spun around to find Carson standing with the widest grin on his lips.

"What are you doing here at this time?" Her gaze flickered to the alarm clock on the nightstand. He was earlier than he'd said he'd be.

"I couldn't wait to see you." He shut the door and came across the room toward her.

It was then she took him in.

Oh my.

The man sure could fill out a nice pair of close-fitting jeans. His dark-navy shirt was crisp with the top button undone. He'd folded the sleeves to expose his forearms. He'd gotten a haircut, but the tips still curled slightly. Demi wanted to run her fingers through it. It was thick but soft, and she'd had plenty of practice the other night.

"I missed you," she murmured.

He gathered her into his arms and brought her flush against him. His head lowered, and he didn't waste any time claiming her lips.

Demi leaned into the kiss. It had been a full twenty-four hours since she'd seen him. His tongue swept into her mouth, teasing hers. They explored each other in slow, gentle stokes.

Carson broke the kiss to trail soft ones along her jawline and down to her neck.

"Carson, we should go. The wedding will be starting soon." She gasped. His hardness pressed into her belly, eliciting a response from her body. It wouldn't take much for the towel surrounding her to fall to the floor.

Carson paused, his warm breath dancing along her skin as he exhaled.

"Parker would kill me if I was late." He chuckled, lifted his head, and cupped her face with his hand. The navy color of his shirt highlighted his gray eyes that studied her. "You might just be worth it."

"We are not going to be late to your brother's wedding." She giggled, pulled away from him, and turned back to her dresser. She picked out lace black thongs and a matching strapless bra, then headed over to the bed.

She took off the towel, smiling at the sound of Carson's sharp inhale of breath. She pulled the thong on before putting on the bra.

"That's what you're wearing underneath the dress?" Carson's voice was strained.

She looked at him over her shoulder.

"Yeah, what's wrong with it?" she asked curiously.

He coasted a hand through his hair, shaking his head. An appreciative gleam appeared in his eyes.

"How the hell am I supposed to concentrate today knowing that is what is underneath that dress?" He walked over to her, reaching for her.

She spun around and rested a hand on his chest.

"Nope. We have to go. You go sit in the chair over there." Demi pointed to the one in the corner by the window.

"What?" He feigned as if he were hurt. "You don't trust me?"

"Not at all. We'll end up there." She gestured to the bed. "And we don't have time for that."

"There's always time for that." A sly grin spread across his face.

"Carson!" she exclaimed, backing up as he moved forward. "I just did my hair, and Maddy will be expecting us. Unless you want to get her upset."

He froze in place and stared at her. He rolled his eyes. "No, I don't want my future sister-in-law mad at me. She's a very scary woman with all of those pregnancy hormones floating in her mind right now."

He sat on the edge of the bed instead and drew an invisible cross on his chest. It was strange how they had only known each other for a week, but it seemed as if it was forever. Demi was comfortable with Carson. They hadn't had a conversation yet about where their relationship was going.

She was a little nervous to talk about what was between them. What if he was using her time here as a fling? Was she only a fuck buddy and a plus-one for his brother's wedding? Would he be okay with that? Eventually she would have to bring it up. She wasn't getting those type of vibes from him, but she had to know what to expect from their time together.

"Behave, Mr. Brooks." Demi found that she couldn't stop smiling. As much as she would love diving between the sheets with him, they had a wedding to attend. She slid the dress on and finished putting her outfit together.

"Ready?" Carson asked. He pushed up off the bed and walked over to her.

She smiled at him and held out her hand. His larger one engulfed hers.

"I want to surprise Maddy with a gift," she admitted.

"Yeah, with what?" Carson asked.

She shrugged and guided him from the room. "At the reception, I want to sing a song for them. Do you think they would mind?"

"I think Parker could figure out getting you to sing the first dance." He shook his head.

"That would be perfect, but are you sure they would want that?"

They walked down the stairs to the lower level. Jaimie and Hakim must have let Carson in the house before going to run some errands, leaving her alone in the house.

"Maddy is your biggest fan. She'd kill Parker if he

didn't. The DJ was going to play a song, so it's not like you are bumping someone special from singing."

Maddy didn't want to go to the wedding empty-handed. She hadn't known what to buy the happy couple, and singing a song for their first dance would be a gift they would be able to cherish for a lifetime.

Demi was glad she wore the hat. The sun was out in full force, and it was great to have to shield her eyes from the glare. Her large sunglasses helped protect her eyes and disguise her identity.

There were rows of chairs in the field where Parker and Maddy would be married. Someone had definitely gone above and beyond to make the area a beautiful country-themed event.

A gazebo was constructed where the couple would share their vows. It set the tone of a rustic country wedding. Blue and gold decorated the area. Along the white chairs that were set out, gold or blue ribbons adorned them.

Demi had to be sitting on the side of the groom.

Almost every chair was taken. There were plenty of people present to bear witness to the union.

There was an older gentleman sitting in the row before her who closely resembled Parker, Wade, and Carson. He had to be their father.

As if sensing her staring, he twisted and glanced back at her. Their gazes met, and he had the same stormy-gray eyes as Carson and his brothers. There was a curious look to him, but he didn't say anything.

Demi returned his nod. A dark-haired woman sitting next to him nudged him, taking his attention from Demi.

Demi blew out a deep breath and glanced around at the crowd. Light music was being played by a few people off to the side of the gazebo. A violinist, a bassist, and a fiddler. The blending of the song with the instruments was absolutely breathtaking.

Demi found herself slowly rocking to the music.

Soon, the pastor made his way to the gazebo. He was dressed in jeans and a button-down shirt. He wore a wide-brimmed hat and clutched a Bible to his chest. He smiled at the crowd.

A few minutes later, Wade, Carson, and Tyler walked down the aisle and took their places. Tyler had a grin on his face. His hair was curly and was freshly trimmed.

Demi had to give it to the Brooks family. They had some fine-looking men in their family. The genes were strong.

Laughter and jokes could be heard. Demi eased around and spotted a few guys chuckling at Parker while he made his way down the aisle. The three of them shared similar features to the Brooks brothers.

Were they additional family? They had the same brown hair as Carson and his siblings, but she couldn't be sure who they'd be.

Parker was dressed in dark-blue jeans and a white button-down shirt with a camel blazer. A white Stetson sat on top of his head. He was all smiles joining his brothers and son. He shook hands with the paster before taking his place next to his son. Tyler, the best man, appeared as if he was serious about this position.

Demi smiled. She was sure the kid was ecstatic that his parents were finally getting married. The music playing changed. Demi watched three women dressed in one-shoulder royal-blue, high-waisted dresses. A floppy bow rested along the women's shoulders.

They were all gorgeous. Large smiles graced their

faces as they held their sunflower bouquets and made it to where they were to stand. A gentle breeze blew, giving them a little comfort from the warmth in the air.

The song morphed into another. A woman came to a mic that was near where the instrumentalists were seated. She began singing a beautiful song in a high soprano. The words spoke of finding that one true love, and Demi smiled.

She glanced over at Carson and found his gaze on her. She winked at him, unable to take her eyes off him. He was dashing in his dark shirt and jeans.

He tossed her a wink, and her grin grew.

Her heart fluttered at his stare. Demi had never responded to any other man this way. She was addicted to Carson Brooks.

What was she going to do when it came time for her to leave?

She paused.

Why did dread fill her at the thought of leaving this small town?

The song came to an end with applause from the audience. Demi joined in, shifting her attention to where everyone was looking.

People began to stand, so she joined them. A young man in jeans, a plaid shirt, and a leather wide-brimmed hat walked up to the mic and sang a cappella. The words of *Thinking Out Loud* by Ed Sheeran flowed from his lips.

Demi was captivated by his voice. It held a slight twang but was smooth as butter.

Maddy was radiant in her white wedding gown. It was made of vintage lace, with off-the-shoulder straps. It was sheer lace adorned with a feathery design. The open back added to the sex appeal. Her long flowing veil trailed behind her with each step she took down the aisle. The woman with her was of similar build and had to be her mother, outfitted in a silver dress.

Maddy and her mother arrived at Parker. She placed Maddy's hand in Parker's. The older woman whispered something to Parker who grinned.

Maddy and Parker faced each other while the young man continued to serenade them with Ed's song.

Demi's eyes blurred. She didn't really know Maddy or Parker, but she could tell something had passed between them. It didn't take a genius to see that they had been through some things.

Love radiated from Parker as he stared down at Maddy. He kissed her hand, then winked at her.

Demi felt honored to be sharing this moment with them.

"You may now be seated," the pastor announced, once the gentleman had reached the end of the song.

Applause went around for him. Demi clapped, having enjoyed his voice.

"It's a beautiful day for these two lovebirds to get married. Would you agree?"

Demi took her seat and felt a twinge of jealousy.

When would she get her happy ending?

She had been so focused on her career that she hadn't really thought of settling down, starting a family with someone who was meant for her. She was thirty years old and wasn't getting any younger.

What she was witnessing, she wanted.

She wanted a man to look at her the way Parker was looking at Maddy.

She blew out sigh, her gaze roaming the bridal party until it landed on Carson. As if feeling her attention on him, he glanced her way.

Her heart skipped a beat when their eyes met.

Was he the one?

THE RECEPTION WAS GOING STRONG. LOTS of alcohol, music, and dancing. Carson had to give it up to Parker for the shindig. The reception was housed in a massive tent placed on Blazing Eagle property. The white construction was decorated with blue and gold. If Carson didn't know any better, he would have thought he was at a palace somewhere, not their ranch.

A band played music in the corner. On the constructed dance floor, people swayed to the beat, while others were scattered around sitting at the tables.

Parker was finally married.

Carson was proud and happy for his brother. He'd married the woman of his dreams, and now there was no looking back for them.

One down, two to go.

Soon, Wade would be up next. He and Joy were planning a small ceremony with just family and a few friends.

Carson leaned back against the bar and took in the party while waiting for the drinks he'd ordered for him and Demi. His gaze landed on her. She was speaking with a member of the band. He took in her dress, and she was absolutely gorgeous. From the moment they had arrived at the reception, guests had been stopping her for her autograph and photos. Being the sweet person she was, she posed for every picture.

"Who's the gal you brought as a date?" Jonah asked, sliding in next to Carson.

Carson glanced over at his father. The elder Brooks was looking his best. He'd gone into town, got a haircut and some new duds. Somehow, Jonah appeared younger. Carson was sure it had something to do with Eliana. Eliana was never far from Jonah's side. Carson was dying to ask his father about the relationship between his father and his nurse, but he knew not to poke a resting bear.

"Her name is Demi," Carson replied.

"Where'd you meet her?" Jonah's gray-eyed gaze landed on him.

Carson watched Demi laugh at something the guy said. A slight tinge of jealousy appeared in his chest.

"Wade and I had stopped for lunch. Ran into her and her sister. We helped them find a good place to eat and ending up taking lunch together."

"I hear she's someone famous. A singer." Jonah nodded toward Demi.

"Yeah, she is." Carson nodded, too.

She moved back over to their table and took her seat.

"Here you are."

The bartender arrived behind Carson.

"Thanks."

Carson swiveled around and reached for his wallet. He took out some cash and tossed it on the counter to tip the guy. He pulled the flutes to the edge of the counter.

"Thanks." The bartender swiped up the money and slid it in his apron. He switched his attention to Jonah. "Can I get you anything, sir?"

Jonah placed his order, turning to Carson once the bartender stepped away to make his order.

"She's a pretty girl," Jonah mentioned.

Carson's eyebrows jerked up high. He picked up the two flutes of champagne and grinned at his father.

"Oh, I know." He winked at Jonah and walked away. The sound of Jonah's chuckle floated in the air behind him.

Carson navigated through the crowd and arrived at their table. Wade and Joy were supposed to be at their table but were nowhere to be found.

"I thought you got lost." Demi smiled when he took his seat at the table next to her.

He slid his chair closer to her, needing to be near her.

"What? And leave you?" He grinned, handing her one of the flutes. "If I'm disappearing, you're going with me." He wagged his eyebrows at her.

She giggled at him. "Champagne? What are we celebrating?"

He leaned back in his seat and rested an arm on the back of her chair. Her body swayed toward him while they both held their glasses up to each other.

"We are celebrating a lot," he murmured. He stared into her eyes, his smile slowly fading.

"We are?" She raised her perfectly sculpted eyebrow. Curiosity filled her gaze as she watched him.

"Oh yes." His fingers played with the dark strands of her hair. "We are celebrating love today. A beautiful couple tied the knot about an hour ago. We are here on a date together—"

"This is a date?"

"I can't be doing this right if you have to question that we are on a date." Carson scoffed.

Demi fell into a fit of giggles at his facial expression.

"I'm just playing." Demi rested a hand on his

thigh. She held her flute up closer to his. "I agree. We have plenty to celebrate. Starting with us."

Carson raised his flute to Demi's, lightly tapping it. He leaned over and pressed a soft kiss on her lips.

"To us," he murmured, his lips brushing hers.

They took a sip of the bubbly drink. Something just passed between them. Carson wasn't sure what, but he knew that there was something to the 'us' toast.

"Ms. Day, we're ready for you. The couple just arrived." The band member Demi had been speaking with earlier now stood by her.

"Thanks, Chris." Demi smiled at him. She tossed back the rest of the champagne and grinned at Carson. She took her hat off and sat it on the empty chair next to her. "I'm a little nervous."

"You'll be fine." He planted another quick kiss to her lips before she stood and walked away toward the band. Carson wondered what song she was going to sing. He had shared with Parker that she wanted to surprise Maddy with singing the song to their first dance. Parker was on board immediately. Maddy was going to get a kick out of this. They had gone off to take some pictures before planning to join the reception.

The emcee announced that Parker and Maddy had

finally arrived. Cheers went around as the happy couple made their way to the dance floor. Carson finished off his drink and stood, ambling over to where the crowd had formed a circle around his brother and his new wife. They were greeting everyone. Maddy looked radiant, and Parker was all smiles. They walked around the circle then joined each other.

Carson pushed forward so he could have a front row seat of his brother about to make a fool of himself.

Brooks men didn't dance.

Parker whispered something in Maddy's ear. Her eyes grew wide, and her head whipped around to the band just as Demi stood front and center.

"Hello, everyone." Demi held the mic with a warm smile on her lips. "I'm Demi Day, and according to the bride, I'm one of her favorite singers."

"Oh my God," Maddy cried out.

Parker laughed and wrapped his arm around her.

Maddy danced in place, giggling. "You are!"

"Well, I just happened to be in town and ran into Maddy. Long story short, I got an invite to the wedding." Demi laughed. A few chuckles went around with her. "Since it was last-minute, I didn't have time to find a gift to buy, so it will be my honor to serenade my amazing fan on her wedding day."

"I love you, Demi," a female shouted in the crowd.

Demi smiled and waved in her direction.

"Maddy and Parker, congratulations on your marriage. May it always be filled with love and good times. This one is for you." The first chord played, and Demi morphed into a beautiful siren before his eyes.

She was meant for the limelight. She had a way about her where everyone fell in love with her.

Tears were running down Maddy's face, and she turned into Parker's embrace.

Demi's voice was smooth, clear, and powerful. She sang Tim McGraw's popular song, *It's Your Love*. Her Texas roots were coming through. Her voice was beautiful, and Carson didn't ever want her to stop.

Carson could barely tear his eyes from the sight of Demi. She sang with such emotion, there wasn't a dry eye as everyone watched Parker and Maddy dance.

Carson swallowed hard.

Her velvety voice washed over him. From a reason unbeknownst to him, he wanted her to sing a song to him.

He ran a trembling hand along his face. They had just met, and already he was envisioning her singing to him as if they were to be together. His gut was trying to tell him something.

She's the one.

There was no doubt about it. Carson Brooks was a stubborn man, and he wanted Demi. He was ready to do whatever he must to win her over.

His gaze swept over the room, taking in everyone swaying and singing along with the song. Parker looked over at him and offered a wink. Carson saluted his eldest brother. He and Maddy deserved their happy ending.

Carson switched his attention to Demi and met her gaze.

Now he had to work on his.

❧ 13 ❧

"Nina," Demi cried out, opening the front door.

Nina grinned and strode forward, wrapping Demi up in a tight hug.

"It is so good to see you," Nina murmured. She stepped back and studied Demi. Nina was stunning in jeans, a bright-yellow blouse, and tall brown riding boots. The woman was curvy and not afraid to flaunt it. "Yes, country air is doing you some good."

"I have to catch you up. We haven't chatted in a while." Demi grinned.

Nina's immaculately plucked eyebrows rose.

Demi grinned and motioned for her and her husband, Sid, to enter. "Sid, how are you?"

"I'm well, Demi. Thanks for having me." Sid grinned.

Demi closed the door behind them and motioned for them to follow her.

"Do you have a place to stay? We have plenty of room," Demi offered.

"Oh, we couldn't. We're actually on our way to Las Vegas and have the tour bus," Nina said, settling in next to her husband.

"Where's the baby?" Demi asked. She took a seat in the chair near them.

Nina and Sid's daughter was about two years old and was the cutest little girl.

"Savannah's with my sister." Nina chuckled. "We needed a break and didn't want to bring her on the tour bus. The ride was too long. They'll fly out later to meet us in Vegas."

"Not that being on the tour bus gives us privacy," Sid said. He kissed Nina's head, and she rolled her eyes.

"It's the life of a rock star," Nina grumbled.

Demi was all too familiar with the life on the tour bus. Small cramped spaces, with little to no privacy because of the crew that rode along on the bus. Whenever they made it to a city, she requested the best room in a hotel with a huge bed for her to spread out on.

"That's the one part I hate about touring," Demi admitted.

"The suits should be here soon," Nina announced. She got down to business. "We are going to go through exactly what you would need to become independent."

"Nina, you really didn't have to do this."

"I do. As black women in the entertainment business, we have to stick together. I don't want anything, and the expense of the lawyers is my gift to you."

Demi smiled at her mentor.

What would she do without her?

This week was going to be busy for her. Not only was she officially going independent, she was going to finalize her deal with Adore Me.

"I'm ready," Demi confessed. It was like a weight off her shoulders at the admission.

"I'm sorry I'm late." Jaimie breezed into the room.

"You are just in time. Hey, girl!" Nina jumped up and gave Jaimie a hug.

"So what are we discussing?" Jaimie sat on the edge of Demi's chair.

"Taking over the world, of course," Nina snorted and leaned into Sid.

"My wife has a fascination with that." Sid chuckled.

"When the suits get here, we'll began. They should be arriving soon." Nina had her business-woman persona on.

Demi was all about it.

She wanted to be like Nina when she grew up. She was going to sit down and take notes. If Nina believed in her, then she wouldn't doubt herself.

Demi enjoyed getting caught up with Nina and Sid. They were two people who were truly in love with each other. Demi could never get enough of hearing the story of how they'd met. It was almost like a fairy tale love story.

Nina the superstar, and Sid was the knight in shining armor.

Just being in their presence had Demi hoping to one day find that special someone who looked at her the way Sid looked at Nina.

The doorbell rang, ceasing all conversation.

"I'll get it." Jaimie hopped up and ran toward the front door.

"Come on. We can meet in the dining room. I

have plenty of coffee and alcohol. Whichever one we need." Demi stood.

"Let's start with coffee and we'll see how this afternoon goes."

CARSON TROTTED ALONG ON TUCKER AT A steady pace. He was dog-tired. It had been a long day, and he was anxious to take a hot shower to wash the layers of dirt from him.

The barn came in to view, and his gaze landed on a familiar figure standing along the corrals.

Rashad, Karl, and Tyler were working. Tyler was practicing on his roping. The kid had energy for days. Maddy and Parker were on a short honeymoon and would be gone for a few days since she was so close to delivering the baby.

He drew closer, his eyes only on Demi. She was dressed in jeans, a top with a jean jacket, and her boots.

"Howdy, there," Demi called out as he drew closer to her.

"Hey there, superstar." He grinned. He suddenly wasn't as tired as he thought he was. Tucker drew to a halt. Carson dismounted, moving toward her.

Tucker wouldn't move. He was a well-trained horse and could even be clingy sometimes.

Demi had been on his mind all day. He had texted her earlier that morning, and she had shared with him that she had a very important meeting with her lawyers over contracts.

He didn't even want to imagine what that had to deal with. The entertainment world was not something he was familiar with. He liked to stay in his small corner of the world of cattle business.

"I'm a little dirty." He chuckled, arriving at her side.

She rolled her eyes and stood on her tiptoes, kissing his cheek.

"That's okay. I can help you get clean later." She winked.

"Where's your car?" He looked around and didn't see her rental.

"I had Jaimie drop me off."

Carson grinned and took her hand. He wasn't letting her make the offer and not follow through.

"Let me put up Tucker and—"

"Who's your friend?" Jonah walked from the barn over to where Carson and Demi stood.

Carson turned around and faced his father.

Jonah was getting stronger as each day passed.

He was ambulating without the cane and seemed more like his previous self. He had lost some weight from around the middle, and the physical therapy and exercising was doing him some good.

"Hello, sir," Demi murmured.

Carson entwined their fingers, not missing his father's glance at their hands.

"Pop, this is Demi. Demi, this is my father, Jonah Brooks."

"It's a pleasure to meet you." Demi held out her hand, a warm smile on her face.

His father took her smaller one and pumped it in a slow shake.

"That was you singing at my son's reception this weekend," Jonah said, releasing Demi's hand.

"That it was. It was a pleasure to sing for them." Demi stepped back.

"You have a mighty fine voice, girl." Jonah nodded.

Carson froze and stared at his father.

Did Jonah just give someone a compliment?

"Thank you." Demi tucked her hair behind her ear and smiled at his father. "While I'm in town, if you need me to sing for you, just let me know."

Demi winked at him, and if Carson wasn't watching, he wouldn't have believed it.

Jonah Brooks blushed.

"Did you need anything, Pops?" Carson cleared his throat.

"Um, yeah. I was wondering if you wanted to come by for dinner? Eliana is cooking, and you know that woman is trying to fatten me up. I could use some help eating all the food." Jonah ran a hand through his thick hair. He had a sheepish expression. "You can bring Demi if you want."

Demi's gaze turned to Carson, and he was rendered speechless. It had been a while since he had eaten dinner at the main house with his father.

"Yeah, Pop. We'll be there. What time?" Carson glanced down at his watch and saw it was going on six o'clock.

"Dinner should be ready by seven-thirty."

"Then we'll be there. I'm about to run home and get cleaned up."

"See you at dinner." Jonah brushed past him and headed toward Tucker. "I'll get Tucker settled for you."

Carson tugged Demi toward where his truck was parked. He was completely confused. The man who was just speaking with them looked like Jonah Brooks, sounded like him, but he was not acting himself.

"Your dad seems so sweet," Demi murmured, leaning into his arm.

Carson just about choked on his spit. A laugh burst from him, sending tears spilling from his eyes.

"What? Did I say something funny?"

Carson wiped his eyes with the back of his hands, trying to control himself.

"Honey, you haven't been here long enough. Jonah Brooks has never been described as sweet."

"But he invited us—"

"One day I will have to catch you up on how my father was before his heart attack. He's a changed man." Carson led her to his truck and assisted her inside.

He jogged round and hopped in the driver's seat. He started the truck and guided it down the dirt road to his house.

"Jonah Brooks has done some things in his life that would make you cringe," Carson began. He tried not to go down memory lane and scare Demi from his father. Jonah had changed when his wife died. Carson had been young when Grace passed away. His father basically ignored his children. The essentials were always met, but the man was practically absent from Carson's life growing up.

Parker and Wade were his main support through

school and football. His elder brothers made sure he didn't stray from the right path. They were protective and caring. Everything elder brothers should be.

But it would have been nice to have his father there.

It wasn't Parker's or Wade's responsibility to make sure Carson grew up.

"Maybe almost dying did something to him," Demi said softly.

He had given her a brief rundown on the type of man his father was.

"That we all are aware of." Carson blew out a deep breath. He didn't want to sour the mood with his horrible family life. "I even think Eliana has something to do with it, too."

He pulled up to his house and parked the truck in front of the garage.

After Jonah had been discharged from the physical therapy program, it was deemed that he didn't need to have a home health nurse either.

But Eliana was still coming around the Brooks ranch.

"Well, that is sweet if he's trying to change for his family."

Carson shrugged. He killed the engine and exited the vehicle. He walked over to Demi's side and helped her down. He entwined their fingers and guided her over to the back door of his home.

"Enough talk about my father. What are you doing here?" he asked. He let them in, towing her behind him. He toed off his boots. His mother had been dead and gone for years, but he could still hear her screaming at him and his brothers to take their boots off when they came inside.

No telling how much shit you're dragging in this house.

Demi kicked her sandals off and followed him. Carson grew anxious having her there again.

"Well, I had a long day of meetings with lawyers, my team, and a good friend of mine stopped by. I wanted to get out, and my first thought was you."

Carson paused and turned to her, pushing her up against the wall.

"Is that so?" he murmured. His cock strained at his jeans, but he needed to have a shower first. He had been out on the ranch all day and he wouldn't be surprised if grime and dirt coated every inch of him.

It'd been two days since the wedding, and she was never far from his mind.

"Yes. I know I'm only in town for a short while, but I was wanting to really get to know you, Carson." Demi looked at him with her big brown eyes. "I want to make the most of the time I have while I'm in Shady Springs and I want to spend as much of it with you."

Carson leaned down and captured her lips with his. A sigh escaped her, her lips parting, allowing him to slip his tongue inside. He teased hers, coaxing it to duel with his.

Carson drew back, not wanting the kiss to go any further. If he didn't stop now, he'd be taking her right here in the hallway against the wall.

"Shower," he murmured.

Demi grinned. "My offer to help still stands."

He all but dragged her down the hall behind him. They had time to do what he was fantasizing about. Their first time had been in the back of his truck, and it had been amazing.

"I'm wholeheartedly accepting." He laughed.

Her giggle floated through the air as they rushed into his bedroom. Carson lifted his shirt over his head and tossed it on the floor.

He chucked his jeans, too, and spun around, walking backward into the bathroom, taking Demi by the hand.

"We don't have much time." Demi's brown-eyed gaze traveled along his body with the hint of appreciation.

"We are going to make time." He spun around

and strode toward the shower. He flicked the handles, turning the water on. He looked back her, seeing that she still had her clothes on. He motioned to them. "Um, those will get wet in the shower."

Demi laughed. "Who said I was getting in with you? I have nothing to protect my hair."

"What?" He eyed her head, tilting his to the side. "I don't understand."

She ambled over to him with a smirk on her lips. Demi stood before him, her hand resting on his pectoral muscle right above his heart. Her hand slowly trailed down his chest, traveling to his stomach.

"Well, I'm sure you aren't up to date on black women's hair, but I have nothing to do my hair with if it were to get wet."

Her hand stopped at the edge of his boxer briefs. His cock was fully engorged, pressing against the soft material. Her eyes flared with a deep passion that he wanted to unleash.

"So no showering together?" he asked, scratching his head. He bit his lip and calculated what he could do in order for her to get in with him.

Demi backed away and hopped up on the counter. A sexy grin spread across her lips. She pointed at the shower.

"You get in. I watch." She wagged her eyebrows playfully.

"Really?"

"Watching a sexy man wash his body is definitely on my bucket list." She motioned to his shorts. "Take them off, cowboy." Her voice grew husky, and those big brown eyes of hers grew so dark they were almost black.

She wanted to play games.

He had no problem joining in on the fun.

Carson smirked, hooking his thumbs on the edge of his shorts. He pulled them down, his cock springing free.

Demi's quick intake of breath could be heard over the running water. Her gaze skimmed his body and focused on his cock. It was erect, away from him. He kicked his shorts off that had puddled around his ankles.

Moving over to the shower, he walked around the glass wall. His girl wanted a show, he'd give her one.

Demi turned her body toward his, her teeth nibbling on her bottom lip as she watched. Carson winked at her and stood underneath the spray of water.

It ran over him, comforting his aching muscles

after a long day's work. He wiped his face, blinking away the droplets that rested on his eyelashes.

He grabbed his soap from the ledge and ran it along his body.

"Enjoying the show?" he asked.

"Immensely."

Carson flexed his muscles, showing off for her. He faced her and grinned. He slid his soapy hand down to his dick. He stroked it, ensuring it was clean while not breaking the stare-off with Demi.

Wrong move.

His cock got extremely excited, thinking this was going to be a one-person party.

Down, boy.

Demi's gaze dropped back to his activities, and he immediately went over football stats in his head.

A few minutes more and then he'd be picking Demi up and carting her off to the bedroom. He just had to hold out a little longer.

Demi got down from the counter and began removing her clothes.

"I'll meet you in here." She blew a kiss and disappeared from the bathroom.

Carson had to make a Guinness Book Record on the fastest shower known to man. He flipped off the water and reached for his towel. He wiped off and tried to hear sounds of movement in the other room.

Silence.

He wrapped the towel around his waist and exited the bathroom. He paused in the doorway at the sight that greeted him.

Demi was naked, resting on her stomach in the middle of his bed. Her dark hair cascaded around her shoulders while her smooth brown skin appeared soft and supple.

His hands itched to touch her again.

"Took you long enough." She trailed her finger across his comforter.

"Just wanted to make sure I washed all the dirt and sweat off of me."

Carson marched forward, not taking his eyes off Demi. He had to admit she looked perfect in his bedroom.

As if she belonged there.

Carson unwrapped the towel and dropped it on the floor by the bed. He knelt on the mattress and slowly crawled over to her. Demi rolled onto her back. He braced himself over her, his leg sliding along hers. He pushed them open so he settled between them.

His cock brushed her slick opening, and he blew out a deep breath.

"I can't get enough of you," he murmured.

"I'm all yours whenever you want me," she whispered.

Carson growled, swooping down and capturing her lips with his. Her mouth parted, allowing his tongue to enter. He swept in, controlling the kiss.

Carson trailed his hand over her body, dropping down to her breasts. Her full mounds filled his large hand. It was soft and pliable.

His lips skated along her face, pressing hot kisses to her jawline. Her fingers dove into his hair. He continued on his journey until he arrived at her breasts. He captured one taut dark bud with his lips. He suckled the mound into his mouth while massaging the other one.

Demi was cushy and womanly, and the scent of her fueled his desire for her. There was a light floral aroma coming from her, along with the hint of musk.

Carson took his time, giving her breasts all the attention they deserved.

"Are you sure we have time for this?" Demi's breathless words broke through his concentration.

"Yeah. This here is more important," he muttered, his lips brushing her nipple. He glanced and found her staring at him with a small smile on her lips. He prayed she wouldn't want to stop. That would be cruel and unusual punishment.

"Okay."

Carson celebrated internally and blazed a path down her stomach until he reached his destination. He pushed her legs open wide while he settled down the bed with her core open for him.

He dropped kisses on the inside of her thighs. He dipped his finger into her drenched core and could have wept at how wet she was for him.

His cock dug into the mattress. It was erect and ready to dive inside her.

But first, he had to have his appetizer. The dinner at his pop's house could wait. There was nothing there that would be as good as what he had splayed out before him on his bed.

Demi's breaths were coming fast. The anticipation of Carson's mouth on her was building. He loved teasing her. His lips and tongue were on her thighs and were not where she needed them to be.

His finger slipped inside her, and she bit back a cry of frustration.

She was so turned on her body trembled with need.

"Carson," she moaned.

She couldn't ever remember moaning out a lover's name before. There was something about Carson that caused her to just go crazy.

"Hold your horses," he murmured. His warm

breath blew along her slick labia. He spread her folds wide, the cool air kissing her clit.

Demi tightened her fingers in Carson's hair. She had a death grip on his thick locks and was not going to let them go. She needed something to hold on to, for she knew from prior experience he was about to take her on one hell of a ride.

The first flick of his tongue on her clitoris had her back arching off the bed. His free hand pushed her back down. He suckled the swollen nub into his mouth while slipping a finger inside her again. This time he rotated his digit around, pressing it against her walls.

His tongue flicked her bud, sending chills down her spine. He worked her over with his tongue and mouth, leaving her writhing underneath him.

Her chest rose and fell quickly while she tried to breathe in air.

Her hips moved on their own accord. A cry escaped her as the pleasure intensified. She glanced down at Carson, finding him with his eyes open, watching her.

She crested.

A guttural moan escaped her, her body quivering. The power of her orgasm flooded her, washing over her in waves.

Demi relaxed on the mattress, barely able to breathe.

Carson sat back on his knees, fisting his cock. He ran his hand along the length of him. The evidence of her release was present on his chin. He wiped his mouth with the back of his hand. His eyes were dark, filled with desire.

"Carson," she breathed.

He nudged her legs open wider, settling down between them. His teeth slid along her neck. She watched him, loving the feeling of his body covering hers.

"I love seeing you in my bed," he murmured. His lips captured hers in a deep, soul-searing kiss. Moments later, he pulled back to stare at her.

The blunt tip of his cock slid through her folds, teasing her. She whimpered, needing to feel him deep inside her.

"I want to watch you take my cock, Demi."

He held his cock while pushing forward into her. His large mushroom-shaped head slipped into her slick opening. Demi groaned, wanting more.

He kept his attention on them as he delved deeper. Her body opened, taking the full girth of him.

Carson thrust forward, sinking completely into her.

"Demi," he growled. He lifted her right leg, resting his hand on the back of her thigh. He moved slowly, with steady strokes.

Demi threw her head back, shutting her eyes tight. Carson could have his way with her anytime.

Her inner muscles gripped him tight. Carson leaned over her, and she raked her nails along his shoulders, needing something to hold on to.

His hips quickened.

"You're so beautiful when you come. I want you to do it again." Carson gasped.

Demi's eyes flew open. "What? I don't think I can."

Carson paused, lodging himself within her tight channel. His crooked grin spread across his face, and she knew she was in trouble.

"Oh, you can." He pulled back and gave another deep thrust. "And you will."

"Carson," she groaned. She couldn't believe how many times she'd said his name. It was like the only thing she could think of, or the only word her brain could formulate.

"You're so fucking wet for me," he growled, his

hips moving in a steady rhythm again. He slid a hand between them, his finger finding its way to her clit.

Her breath caught in her throat as he massaged her bud.

"Oh my," she gasped, the familiar sensation of her orgasm coming for her. She widened her hips and moved her pelvis in rhythm with his like a wanton hussy.

"Squeeze me," he demanded.

She did as he'd commanded, eliciting a moan from him. The pulse between her legs grew.

He pinched her nub, thrusting harder.

Demi screamed, reaching another climax.

Carson's hips rocked against her.

A roar ripped from him as he poured himself into her. Demi wrapped her arms around him, holding him close. His body trembled, his warm breaths skating across her shoulder while his semisoft cock remained lodged within her.

Demi closed her eyes, feeling at home.

"I DIDN'T THINK Y'ALL WOULD BE COMING," Jonah mumbled, eyeing down at his watch.

"Well, Pop, I didn't want to come over stinking of

the ranch so I needed to get washed up." Carson tugged Demi into the house after him.

His father gave him an all-knowing look. He glanced at Demi then back to Carson, releasing a snort.

"Whatever." The elder Brooks waved for them to follow him. "Come on, now. Eliana just set the table."

Carson peeked over at Demi who had the expression of someone who'd got caught with their pants down around their ankles. He bit back a joke. They were a little late, and for a good reason.

He couldn't keep his hands off her.

The sex between them had been out of this world. Demi fit perfectly around him, and he never wanted to escape from her warm, slick cocoon.

Just thinking of their lovemaking had him growing stiff again.

He closed the front door, following behind his father. He wrapped an arm around Demi's waist, his hand sliding down to her ass.

She jerked her gaze to him, her eyes wide.

"What are you doing?" she mouthed.

He grinned, leaning down close to her ear. "Helping you to the dining room, superstar."

She giggled and tried to elbow him away from

her. He playfully brought her closer to him, his hand remaining where it was. They entered the dining room in a fit of giggles and laughter.

"All right, you two." Jonah motioned to the kitchen. "Wash up before you sit down at this dinner table."

Eliana was in the kitchen standing at the stove, stirring something in a large pot.

"Smells good in here," Demi mentioned.

Eliana turned around with a wide smile. "Thank you. I'm Eliana."

She walked over to Demi with her hand outstretched.

"I'm Demi." She took Eliana's hand and shook it.

"Oh, I know who you are. My granddaughter is a big fan of yours. She has a poster of you on her wall. That's the only way I really recognized you." Eliana laughed.

"Really? I would love to meet her sometime." Demi grinned.

"Oh, she would love that."

"I don't get a greeting?" Carson teased.

Eliana jerked in place as if she'd just seen him. "Oh, hush up, boy. You're here all the time. Having a celebrity over for dinner is not something we do every day." She batted at him with her hand.

Eliana was a sweetheart who had nerves of steel to put up with Jonah Brooks. She was good for his father. He and his brothers were thankful for finding her. She was pretty, and he could see why his father was smitten with her.

Brooks men had a weakness for beautiful women.

"While I'm here in Shady Springs, I'm just Demi." Demi moved over to the sink and washed her hands.

"Hurry up and clean up. Dinner will be cold soon. I'm sure Carson is your reason for being late for dinner." Eliana winked at him before leaving the kitchen.

His face grew warm.

He moved over to the sink and trapped Demi with his hands braced on both sides of her.

"Wait your turn." Demi bumped her butt back into him.

He grinned and leaned down, nuzzling his face into the crook of her neck. He slipped his hands onto her sides and tickled her, eliciting a stifled scream.

"When can I have another turn?"

She jumped out of his arms and flung water at him.

"They are waiting for us." She spun around and

grabbed a paper towel to dry her hands. "I'll be in there with Eliana and your father."

She escaped the room, leaving him chuckling.

Carson stepped to the sink and quickly washed his hands then joined the others in the dining room. In the back of his mind, he wondered if there was any special reason for his father to invite them to dinner.

He couldn't even remember the last time they'd all had dinner at the house.

The scent of delicious homecooked food called to him. Carson wasn't the best cook but could get by.

"Hurry up, boy. You already made us wait for your arrival—"

"Jonah Brooks," Eliana snapped. Her head tilted to the side as she stared his father down.

Oh, yeah. Jonah Brooks had met his new match.

Carson grinned and took his seat next to Demi.

"I'm hungry, woman," Jonah grumbled.

"Well, a few minutes wouldn't hurt you. You're always complaining I'm fattening you up." Eliana smiled at them.

There was a sheepish expression on Jonah's face, and Carson had the urge to take his cell out of his pocket to snap a picture. Neither of his brothers would believe him if he told them about this.

"Now bless the food, Jonah," Eliana said.

Now Carson was floored.

Meals at the Brooks house had been different when he was growing up. The boys had sat at the kitchen table to eat while their father took his meal in his recliner in front of the television.

When his mother had been alive, Carson remembered them all eating together at the table like a family.

But once Grace had died, their father left them be.

Jonah said a short and direct prayer, then they were allowed to eat.

Carson was in awe at how well the meal went. Demi brought a smile to the old man's face a few times. Eliana was bustling with questions.

"For you to have just met not too long ago, you two appear really close." Eliana motioned to the two of them.

Carson leaned back and rested his arm along the back of Demi's chair. They shared a look.

"We just clicked," he replied. It was the truth. From the moment he'd laid eyes on her, he'd felt something.

"I agree. Carson is a great guy, and I've enjoyed spending time with him." Demi gently elbowed him.

He drew her to him, dropping a kiss on her forehead.

"Well, what's going to happen when it's time for you to leave Shady Springs?" Jonah asked. His gray eyes settled on them.

The room grew silent.

There's the Jonah Brooks Carson knew.

He bit back the urge to roll his eyes. His father just had to go and ruin a fun evening.

"We hadn't thought that far ahead," Demi said, her smile fading. Her gaze flicked to Carson before turning back to Jonah. "But I guess we will cross that bridge when it comes."

"That we will." Carson put his hand on her shoulder to give her comfort.

Something passed on her face that he couldn't place.

She was worried about something.

"Long distance can be hard, and you're a singer traveling all over the world. How would you have time for my boy? A family?" Jonah asked.

"That's enough questions, Jonah," Eliana cut in. She placed a hand on his forearm, shaking her head. "They are adults and both highly intelligent. I'm sure they will figure out what is best for them."

"Here, let me help clear the table." Demi stood abruptly.

"Oh, you don't have to. I can get it," Eliana said.

"No, ma'am. My mother would have my hide if I didn't help clean up after being fed." Demi took Carson's plate and stacked it on top of hers.

"We'll do it together." Eliana stood and began helping Demi.

They carried what they could into the kitchen.

Carson waited until the women were out of earshot.

"You happy with yourself?" Carson zeroed in on his father. He knew Jonah was going to find a flaw in Demi. It was his nature to ruin anything that could be considered good for his boys.

"I was just asking questions like any good father would do." Jonah met his unwavering gaze head-on.

"Good father?" Carson snorted. Maybe Jonah did have some brain damage from the heart attack. "You've got to be fucking kidding me."

"I did the best by you boys."

"Seriously? That was your best?" Carson leaned forward, resting his forearms on the table. "I'd hate to see you at your worst then."

"Who bailed your sorry asses out of jail anytime you got arrested? Put clothes on your back? Food on the table? Worked from sunup to sundown so you could get all the equipment you needed for football?" Jonah slammed his fist down on the table.

"Jonah, your blood pressure," Eliana said quietly from the doorway.

Jonah held up a hand, not taking his eyes off Carson.

"Well, I'm sorry I was ever a bother." Carson pushed back from the table and stood, ignoring his father's curses.

"Was I a pissy father? I'll be the first to admit that," Jonah exploded. He stood from the table to his full height. "Your mother died, leaving me alone to raise three boys. I knew nothing of being a father. Your mother did everything. She was *my* everything and she was taken from me. From us."

Carson ran a trembling hand along his face. He swallowed hard, emotions swirling in his chest.

"I did only what I knew to do. Provide." His father's voice grew quieter. He looked away, staring out the dark window. The tension in the room was palpable. "You boys never wanted for anything. I made damn sure of it."

Carson cleared his throat, willing the tears that threatened to not spill. Speaking of his mother was like ripping an old Band-Aid off.

Eliana stood frozen in the doorway.

Carson had been in junior high when she'd passed. Her absence was felt in the Brooks family. She had been the glue, the sunshine; any way you wanted to spin it, Grace Brooks had been it.

But Jonah just hadn't understood that his three boys who were motherless, needed their father to step up.

"Pop—"

"No, you hear me out. When I was hospitalized, something changed in me. Waking up and seeing you boys there, it made me realize what I had in front of me this entire time." Jonah walked around the table and came to stand before Carson. He rested a hand on Carson's shoulder and looked him square in the eye. "I'm sorry for everything I didn't do right in your life. You've grown up to be a fine man, and I'm trying to change."

Carson was rendered speechless.

He stared at the man who had raised him and could only nod.

It had taken a lot for Jonah to apologize to him for the shitty childhood, but could Carson really forgive his father?

❧ 15 ❧

Demi sat on the stairs of the Brooks home and stared at the stars. She had left the dining room, uncomfortable with the reality that Jonah had reminded her of. She was going to be leaving Shady Springs.

She knew that.

But it almost hurt to hear someone else say it.

What she and Carson had was good.

Better than good.

She wanted to explore it. Long-distance relationships could work. There were plenty of people who were successful at it.

Blowing out a deep breath, she brought her knees up to her chest and wrapped her arms round them. She'd traveled the world and found many places she loved visiting, but there was something about Shady Springs.

Or it could be a certain cowboy.

The screen door opened behind her. Demi knew without looking that it was Carson. He came to stand in front of her.

"Are you all right?" he murmured.

"Yeah." She sniffed.

"My old man doesn't have a filter." He rummaged a hand through his hair. Frustration lined his voice. "I'm sorry."

"It wasn't what he said." She stood and walked down the few stairs. Her arms found themselves wrapped around her as she strode over to his truck.

"Well, what was it?"

Her eyes were drawn again to the stars. She was being pulled in so many directions at the moment it was like the weight of the world was on her shoulders.

A warm presence came up behind her. Demi turned around and stared into Carson's eyes. She bit her lip to keep from screaming her frustration. He cupped her face, trailing his thumbs along her skin.

"Tell me, Demi. What's bothering you?"

She inhaled a shaky breath, her body leaning into his.

"There is just so much going on with my career right now, and I'm having the time of my life here in Colorado with you." The words rushed out of her mouth. She was barely able to stop herself. "But your father is right. Soon I'll have to leave here, and that means leaving you."

His soft caress on her face calmed her nerves slightly. Her pulse pounded in her ears.

Carson leaned down, settling his lips gently on hers.

"Well, let's make the best of this time we have." He dropped another kiss on her lips.

She parted hers slightly, allowing his tongue to slip inside. The man kissed her to within an inch of her life.

Her body sagged against his, her legs barely able to hold her up.

"Carson," she groaned, her lips brushing his.

He pulled back. The intensity of the heat in his eyes could be clearly seen.

She didn't know what tomorrow or next week would bring. Her lease wasn't up yet. She had another month to go on it but she had to fly back to LA for business. The meeting with the lawyers and Nina had gone perfectly, as planned. They were going to be meeting with the label and officially cutting ties with them.

She was going to be her own boss now.

Her own label.

Distributing her music independently.

It was a once-in-a-lifetime opportunity, but it was scary.

While in LA, she had a meeting lined up with the cosmetic company.

Everything in her life was falling into place, just as she dreamed it to be.

Only, she'd never imagined she would meet Carson.

"Tell me what you need." Carson's deep voice grew husky. His hands traveled along her waist and down to her ass. He cupped her to him, pushing his hardness against her stomach.

"You," she whispered. She trailed her hand down his chest, gripping his shirt. "I want you to make me forget the world. I only want it to be me and you."

A growl erupted from Carson's chest. He took her hand and practically dragged her to his truck. He helped her in and shut the door, leaving her in silence. Her gaze followed him as he walked around the vehicle. He got in and started the truck. The engine roared to life.

He turned the truck around and hit the gas. The tires screeched, tossing up dirt behind them. The truck took off down the dirt road, leading them back to Carson's house.

Demi sat back, staring at Carson.

She wasn't sure if it was possible, but deep down she knew she was completely and utterly in love with Carson Brooks.

CARSON CAME OUT OF THE CLOSET, DRESSED and ready for work. It was the weekend, but that didn't mean he was off. He was a Brooks, and there were always things that needed to be done on the ranch. Ranchers didn't work Monday through Friday.

His father had instilled one thing into him and his brothers.

Their work ethic.

He walked over to the bed, his gaze landing on Demi, who was still asleep. Her naked form was thankfully covered by the sheet.

Last night outside his father's house, she had looked to him with the most haunted eyes he'd ever seen.

Demi was a strong woman, and she'd reached out to him, needing him to chase away whatever was bothering her.

Their lovemaking had been desperate. He carried the scratches on his back as proof. He'd carry them with honor. His girl had been a sexy kitten—tiger—last night.

Carson sat on the edge of the bed beside her. She slept on her side, her dark hair covering her face. He reached over and brushed it away. Her warm brown skin was soft, her lips still swollen from their kisses.

A sigh escaped her, and he prayed she would sleep a little longer.

Leaning over, he lightly kissed her forehead.

He'd give anything to crawl back into the bed with her.

But work called.

"What time is it?" her husky voice broke through his thoughts.

"Five-thirty." He trailed his hand through her hair, pushing it farther from her face. "Stay and get some rest. There's plenty of coffee and food. I should be back by noon."

She rolled over, the sheet sliding dangerously low. A sexy grin spread along her lips.

"You sure you have to go?"

Unable to resist, he bent his head down and captured her lips in a slow, heated kiss. It took all of his strength to pull away from her.

"I'm sure. There are some animals who need to be feed and will be really ornery if I don't bring their food on time."

"Why don't I come with you." Demi moved to sit up, but he pressed her back down.

"No, you need the rest."

"I don't. I want to see what you do." She brushed his hand away and sat up, the sheet finally falling away to reveal her beautiful brown breasts.

She was using her feminine wiles to get what she wanted.

Demi Day didn't fight fair.

Carson cleared his throat, unable to look away from the beautiful masterpieces in front of him.

"You should, um…" He had forgotten his train of thought. Running a hand along his face, he began to remember.

She wanted to come out on the ranch with him.

"You can wear one of my shirts," he offered.

Her squeal pierced the air. She threw herself at him, wrapping her arms around his neck. She squeezed him hard in a hug.

"It won't take me long to get ready." She rolled out of the bed and ran to the bathroom.

With a chuckle, Carson pushed off the bed and stood. He went down to the kitchen to put on some coffee. If Demi was going to be working hard on the ranch this morning, she was going to be needing plenty of caffeine.

Footsteps on the stairs drew his attention. Demi skipped into the kitchen; his heart skipped a beat.

She had put her hair in two French braids, making her appear younger. She had gone in his closet and found one of his plaid shirts. It was too big on her, but she made it look so sexy. It was tied at her waist, and the sleeves were folded up. Her jeans molded to her, showcasing her curves.

How the hell was he supposed to work with her dressed like that?

"What do you think?" She playfully modeled her outfit.

"Beautiful." He chuckled.

She skipped over to him and wrapped her arms around his waist.

"I'm glad you think so." She stood on her tiptoes and kissed his chin. "You, sir, need a wardrobe upgrade."

"What's wrong with my clothes?" He laughed.

"You have so many of the same shirts, but different colors." She giggled.

"I'm a simple man. What can I say?" He shrugged.

"There is nothing simple about you, Carson Brooks." She wagged a finger at him, stepping away from him.

"How do you take your coffee?"

"Cream and sugar, please." She batted her eyelashes. "What's for breakfast?"

He frowned. He hadn't thought about feeding her before they left to start work. Most days he didn't eat breakfast first, but would have a good lunch.

He scratched his head and looked around the kitchen.

"What do you want?"

"Toast would be fine." She took a seat at the island.

He moved around the kitchen with a grin on his lips. He hadn't prepared breakfast for a woman in a long time. Demi sat patiently as he got her toast and buttered it. She ate it while he prepared their coffee in paper traveler mugs he kept in stock.

Soon they were in the truck and headed to the main barn.

"Ready to become a cowgirl?" He glanced over at her.

She took a sip of her coffee, then nodded. "Sure am."

"Well, all right then." He chuckled, then focused back on the road. A few of the hands usually came in on the weekend. They rotated weekends to be fair.

"So what are we going to do first?" she asked.

"We're going to check on the horses, then go out and check on the herd."

He guided the truck over to the barn and parked. They got out and went inside. There was no sign of his brothers or any of the hands. They must be the first to arrive.

"This reminds me of my childhood." Demi spun around in front of him. She was like a kid in a candy shop.

He followed behind her and snickered. "You grew up on a farm?"

"Nope. When I was a child, our school would take us on field trips to the local farms and ranches. We would get to learn all about agriculture. It was the highlight of school. We would have so much fun."

He caught up to her and took her hand in his.

They strolled through the expansive structures. Some of the horses were curious, sticking their heads out the doorways to see who was in the barn.

"That's sort of how we started Kiddie Camp here. It was a dream of Wade's. He wanted to do something for the local kids. What he thought would only be a few kids turned into a large program."

"That's amazing that you guys do something like that."

"It's rewarding, and we all participate. Parker used to be a bull rider, and the kids love when he comes to do talks with them."

"Seriously?" Demi's eyes grew round. "Like those big, mean bulls that try to throw you off and stomp you in the ground?"

"Yup. The one and only."

"Oh my. I've been to a rodeo once and watched a guy get thrown from one. The clowns had to intervene to protect him."

Carson grimaced. His brother's career-ending injury had been about the same thing, only the bull had it out for Parker. It had landed right on Parker's knee, shattering it.

His career was over, and his limp was a daily reminder of what had happened. He'd had surgery after surgery to fix his knee, but he still limped.

Thankfully, he had the ranch to come home to.

It wasn't the glamorous life he used to lead, but now Parker was better off here on the ranch and married to Maddy.

"Come on. Let's put you to work, cowgirl." He reached up and tugged on her braid.

"Tell me what to do."

He couldn't resist drawing her in close and kissing her. He controlled the kiss, resting his hands on the sides of her face.

A cough sounded behind them. Carson lifted his head to find Darnell and Stan walking into the barn.

Demi wrapped an arm around his waist and turned toward them.

"We have a new hand?" Stan said.

"I hope not. I'm sure she will want to file a complaint with human resources." Darnell snorted.

"Ha, ha." Carson rolled his eyes. "You're both late."

"How would you know? You're too busy making kissy faces with her." Darnell grinned.

"Get to work," Carson growled.

They were good men and currently busting his ball. He glanced down at Demi who was smiling.

"Hey, fellas." She gave them a small wave.

They came to stand in front of Demi and Carson.

"Boss, you putting her to work?" Stan asked.

"She wanted to see what it is we do." Carson shrugged. He wrapped arm around her shoulders and pulled her in. "We're going to make an honorary cowgirl out of her by noon."

‹ 16 ›

The last two days had been very tiring. Demi had worked alongside Carson on the ranch. She now had a new respect for ranchers. She knew their job was hard and taxing on the body, but now she had firsthand experience.

She moved around her room slowly, packing a small bag. They would be flying back to California for a few days.

As much as she didn't want to go, she had to. If she was going to cut ties with her record label, it would have to be done in person. Jaimie had also booked her meeting with Adore Me while she was in town.

She had a month left on her lease and she planned to come back to Shady Springs to enjoy it. Not only did she love the little town, but there was another reason she was wanting to return.

Carson.

A smile graced her face. She had to rush to finish packing. A few members of her team had arrived here to escort her back to LA. Janet, her stylist, had laid clothes down on her bed and had already got her hair together. Janet had performed a miracle as she always did. Demi walked past the mirror on the wall and paused.

This was superstar Demi, as Carson would say.

Her makeup was done flawlessly, her hair was thick and long, thanks to the wig custom-made for her. Janet had put her hair in a protective style underneath the wig. It was routine so she would be able to have multiple styles for different events all in the same day.

"Shit." She glanced at the clock and moved around, picking up things she wanted to take with her. Demi had yet to get fully dressed, only wearing her silk robe and undies. Janet always knew what Demi loved and ensured she was outfitted in clothing that appealed to her.

She had hoped Carson would be able to see her off. They were catching a private helicopter that would then take them over to Colorado Springs, then fly to California.

"He must not have been able to leave the ranch," she muttered.

The muscles in her legs still ached from all the hard work she'd done at the ranch. Her gaze landed on the four-inch heels sitting pretty on the floor, and she grimaced. Being in Shady Springs, she had gotten used to wearing her boots and sandals.

Carrying her last few items over to her expensive name-brand bag siting on the bed, she tossed them in and zipped it shut.

There was a knock at the door.

"Come in," she called out, not looking over her shoulder. She took in the outfit that Janet had prepared for her and was satisfied with it. Once they were back in LA, she would be whisked from the airport directly to her first meeting. She didn't want to waste any time when she was in town. Meetings would be tight, but it was the way of the business.

A low whistle cut through the air.

Demi spun around to see Carson leaning against the doorjamb with his arms folded in front of him. He was dressed in jeans, a gray long-sleeved t-shirt, and had a baseball cap on his head turned around backwards. He hadn't shaved and had a slight stubble on his face. His smoldering eyes locked on her.

Holy hell.

Could the man get any sexier?

"Carson," she whispered.

"Well, I'll be, superstar. Look at you."

The huskiness in his voice sent a tremor through her body. Her nipples beaded into tight buds and pushed against the robe.

"What about me?" She feigned innocence, looking down at herself. She had been primed and primped once Janet had arrived at the house. She brushed the silky material that stopped mid-thigh.

He pushed off and marched into the room, shutting the door behind him. The faint click of the lock sounded. Her pulse pounded in her ears. She held his heated gaze as he stalked toward her. He reached her, his hands cupping her face. He lowered his head to hers, capturing her lips in a sizzling kiss.

Demi melted into Carson.

The kiss took her breath away. The man had a way about his mouth and tongue that turned her body to a gelatinous puddle. She held on to him, not trusting her legs to keep her up. He walked them backwards until her back touched the wall.

A gasp escaped her at the feeling of his erection

against her stomach. Her core clenched at the memory of him sliding inside her.

Carson leaned his forehead on hers.

"Does that answer your question?" he murmured.

"You have a hell of a way with not using words to get your point across." She glanced up at him, her breaths still coming fast. She caressed the side of his face and smiled. "And I like it."

"You are absolutely beautiful." He studied her face, his gaze dropping down to her black robe. "I'm going to miss you."

Her heart lurched at his admission.

"I'll miss you, too."

His hands tugged on the tie of the robe, revealing her body encased in her dark lace lingerie. Her breasts were pushed up in a high corseted bra, with the matching high-waisted thong. Carson's sharp intake of breath was the only sound in the room.

"I don't know if I can let you go back to California wearing this."

His gaze flicked to hers, and Demi would have sworn her heart stopped. The fire in his eyes had her core dripping. Moisture collected at the apex of her thighs.

"No one else will see this," she whispered. She

dropped her hands to his belt buckle and began undoing it.

"They better not," he growled. He reached up and pushed her robe down her arms. The soft material floated to the floor.

She celebrated internally once she finally got his pants unbuttoned and drew the zipper down. Carson, impatient, crushed his mouth to hers. She became lost in the kiss while she hooked the back of his jeans and eased them down slightly. He helped her, freeing his massive erection.

Before she knew it, Carson had lifted her and pressed her back against the wall without breaking the kiss. He reached between them and moved the small scrap of material covering her pussy to the side, and with one thrust, he was home.

He swallowed her cry of passion. He was deep inside her, stretching her muscles. She was in love with the full feeling he always gave her.

"Hold on, superstar," Carson breathed.

Demi wrapped her arms around his neck, her legs already secured around his waist.

He pulled back and thrust forward again. A moan slipped from her.

She knew that her team was downstairs waiting for her, but she didn't care. She was going to be away from her man for three to four days and deserved a satisfying send-off.

"Are you going to think of me?" Carson nipped her neck, his warm breath sliding along her skin.

"God, yes," she groaned. Demi squeezed her eyes shut, relishing the feeling of him fucking her.

There was no other way to describe it. He'd made love to her before, but this was pure fucking. He was leaving his mark on her.

Not that any other man could hold a candle to him.

He moved faster, sending his cock farther inside her. Demi chanted his name, unable to speak any other word.

She gave herself over to the intense sensations overcoming her. No longer did she control anything with her body. Tremors snuck through her as her climax grew closer.

Carson's groans filled her ear. His warm breath skirted along her neck, and his breaths grew faster.

"Demi," he moaned. "You have to come back to me."

Tears formed in her eyes at the raw emotion in his voice.

This was not a goodbye.

Not by a long shot.

"I will," she gasped. The tears slipped free of her shut eyes and trailed down her cheeks. There had never been anyone who elicited such a response from her. She buried her face into the crook of his neck. "I promise."

He fucked her harder, his cock brushing along her swollen nub, pushing her over the edge. Her muscles tightened, a silent scream ripping from her. Her body writhed with his, the hard orgasm washing over her.

She didn't want to alert everyone in the house as to what she and Carson were doing.

Carson's grip on her tightened painfully on her thighs.

"Fuck," Carson moaned, his motions becoming frantic. His release hit him, and he leaned farther against her, pouring himself into her.

Demi kept her arms and legs curled around him, not wanting to break the spell that fell around them.

Demi blinked the tears away when she opened her eyes. Carson lifted his head and glanced at her.

"Did I hurt you?" he asked, concern lining his features. He gently reached up and brushed her hair from her face. He trailed this thumb along her bottom lip which quivered under his touch.

She shook her head and brought his head to her.

She joined her lips to his, giving him a sweet gentle kiss, pouring all of her emotions for him in it.

In the short amount of time she had spent with him, she'd come to need him. She was never one who believed in instant love, but what she felt for Carson was strong.

It felt right.

She would return.

There wouldn't be anything that would stand in her way from coming back to this man.

CARSON SAT ON THE EDGE OF THE CHAIR and watched Demi finish dressing. He'd arrived at the house in time to see her off. He wouldn't miss this for the world.

Her staff were a little shocked to see him. He'd met her security guard, Lester, and a woman named Janet. Jaimie had introduced him before sending him to find out what was taking Demi so long.

It would be the first time she was leaving him to go back to her real life. He had to admit he was nervous about it.

Carson Brooks had never doubted himself before

until now. He had always been confident and was used to getting what he wanted.

This was a different ballgame.

Would Demi get back to LA and forget about him? He knew she'd said she planned to come back, but things could change.

What if she didn't feel as strongly about him as he did for her?

He shook his head.

That wasn't his Demi.

If she said she was coming back, then she would.

She could not walk away from what was between them. She felt it, too. How her body responded to his wasn't normal.

He hadn't meant to jump her bones when he'd arrived, but seeing her dolled up, her long hair, that sexy robe, sent every cognitive thought he had out the window.

His cock had taken over thinking.

His main mission was to sink deep inside her and remind her of how good the sex was between them.

"I shouldn't be gone that long," she said, sitting on the bed. She was dressed in a long flowing black skirt that billowed around her ankles and a crisp white button-down shirt with sleeves that folded up to reveal her forearms. The collar was wide and rested along her shoulders underneath the dark tresses that flowed on her back.

She slid her small feet into her heels and stood.

"There's no rush," he lied.

Hell yeah, there was. He wanted her back in Shady Springs, and better yet, in his bed.

Forever.

"How do I look?" She twirled around, the skirt floating through the air. A grin spread on her face.

He pushed up and walked toward her. Staring at her, he knew it was Demi, but it wasn't the same Demi he had fallen in love with.

The air was ripped from his lungs.

Love?

Fuck, he wasn't going to try to fight what he was feeling for Demi.

He had fallen in love with the beautiful siren. He wasn't sure what he was going to do about it. He was going to have a few days to figure it out while she was gone.

"Beautiful." His voice ended on a croak. He cleared his throat and reached for her.

She dodged his hand, laughing.

"Oh, no." She wagged a finger at him. "We know what happens when you get that gleam in your eye and reach for me."

He barked a laugh, watching her stride over to pick up her bag. He followed behind her and took it from her.

"Seriously?" He arched an eyebrow at her.

"Do you not remember what happened when you walked into this room?"

"How can I resist?" He captured her wrist and brought her near to him. He leaned down close to her. "That little black robe did nothing to hide how your body reacted to me. Those pretty nipples of yours were calling my name."

A tremor snuck through her.

Good.

It just proved a point.

She may not have realized it, but her body was his.

Demi turned those pretty brown eyes of hers to him. He could get lost in her bedroom eyes easily.

"You can't say things like that, Carson," she breathed.

"Why not?"

Her eyes studied him. Her tongue peeked out and ran along her bottom lip, moistening it. He bit back a groan, wanting to swoop down and nibble on her lips that were still swollen from his kisses.

"Because I—"

They were interrupted by knocking.

"Did ya'll get lost in there?" Jaimie's voice sounded from the other side of the door.

Demi glanced at him, her expression revealing she had more to say, but she turned away and walked over to open up.

"I'm ready," Demi announced.

"I would say what was taking so long, but I can put two and two together." Jaimie eyed the two of them.

"What are you talking about?" Demi reached up and smoothed down her hair. "We were just talking."

"Sure you were. Everyone is ready." Jaimie turned her attention to him. "I told you to find out what was taking her so long."

Carson trailed behind them, hefting the strap of her bag over his shoulder with a grin spreading across his face.

"I did." He winked at her, turning to Demi. "Anything else you need me to carry?" he asked.

"No, that's it. My purse is downstairs. I'm traveling light." She reached for his hand and entwined their fingers.

They followed Jaimie and went downstairs, finding everyone waiting in the foyer.

"It's about time," Lester muttered.

"Oh, hush up. You know it's hard work to get this beautiful," Demi said. Whatever was bothering her before they'd left the room had disappeared from her. She was back to her normal silly self.

Janet handed Demi her purse and paced around her, fixing her hair.

"What happened to your makeup?" Janet sniffed. She glanced at Carson then returned to her task. "I'll fix it when we get to the airport."

"Time to go, people," Jaimie announced. She placed arm around Hakim and guided him out the door first.

They exited the house with Jaimie locking up. There was a black Suburban truck parked out front. Lester began loading the bags into the back of the SUV.

They arrived at the truck with Jaimie, Hakim, and Janet getting inside.

"I'll take that." Lester motioned to the bag Carson carried.

He handed it off to the security guard and turned back to Demi.

"I'll text you as soon as we land in LA," Demi said.

"That's fine," he said.

Lester slammed the truck door and moved to the

driver's door and got in, leaving the two of them outside the vehicle. The engine started, signaling it was truly time for her to leave.

He tilted her chin up, staring in her eyes.

"Come back to me, superstar."

He dropped a sweet, short kiss on her lips. He opened the door and helped her inside the truck. She blew him a kiss, then he shut the door.

Carson backed way, watching the truck drive off with his heart inside it.

Demi walked through LAX with determination in her gait. She was back in LA, and it was time for her to get down to business. Lester stayed close to her, guiding them through the crowded airport.

"We are walking though terminal seven," Lester announced, speaking into his cell phone. Their driver would be waiting for them. "Shit."

Demi tensed and glanced at him. "What's wrong?"

"Paparazzi got wind that you are here." Lester's face grew serious as he hung up. He slid it inside his blazer pocket. He had been with her for years, and she trusted him immensely.

Having paparazzi hunt her down was just a normal part of the job.

"What could they possibly want?" she asked, even though she knew the answer. They didn't have to want anything. They were always sniffing for a story.

"There will be two trucks. One for us, and the other for Janet and Hakim to take them home," Jaimie said, clearly in her manager role. "Rowan is on standby, waiting for the official word."

Demi nodded. Lester was setting a fast pace through the airport. LAX had to be one of the busiest in the world, and there were tons of people. Demi could easily tell who recognized her. She tried to keep her head down, but it was hard to do that and walk.

"Deb will meet us at the label," Jaimie said.

"Good." Deb Boone was her longtime entertainment attorney. She had wheeled and dealed all of Demi's previous contracts for anything that pertained to her business. Demi trusted her to ensure that anything Demi signed would be in her best interests.

"I have a few more men meeting us at the gates to ward off the media." Lester motioned for her turn at the corner. Lester was a former professional footballer who'd played a few years and then moved into the security business for entertainers. He came highly recommended, and during the years he had worked for her, they had become friends.

"Yes, sir." She had to practically run to keep up with his long strides.

He was built like a Mack Truck and was still quick on his feet. Nothing ever got past him. Demi always felt safe in his presence.

"Auntie, will you be coming home today?" Hakim asked.

"After my meetings, I will." She ruffled his hair and grinned at him. "Why do you ask?"

"Because when we were in Shady Springs you didn't come home some nights." He shrugged.

"Hakim!" Jaimie snapped.

"What I say?" Hakim glanced around innocently.

Demi's face warmed when Lester's head jerked toward her. He rested a hand on the small of her back and guided her toward the exit. There were so many people gathered outside the security line. It would be hard to make out who was media and who was not until they got closer.

"Don't give me that look." She chuckled, trying to appear nonchalant.

"You were with that Carson dude?" Lester asked.

"Not that it's any of your business, but yes," she replied loftily.

"You know we need to run a check on him."

"For what?" Demi rolled her eyes.

"You can never be too careful. You are worth a lot of money, my dear. We don't want anyone taking advantage of you," Lester said.

"Carson and his family are very well-off. There is nothing to worry about."

"Yeah, we'll see," he muttered. His grip on her tightened. "There's Kevin. Heads up, ladies and gentleman."

Lester never liked taking her through crowded places. There was a reason he was the best in the business. He stayed glued to her hip as they entered the general area.

"Demi!"

The flash of the cameras lit up.

She instantly put her head down. Lester tried to push through the people trying to get pictures of her. They were like vultures, uncaring what they had to go through to get a shot of her.

"Move out the way," Lester growled, elbowing someone out of the way.

The whirl of cameras snapping shots of her echoed through the air.

Time appeared to slow while they maneuvered through the swarm. Finally, they arrived outside.

There were two black SUVs waiting for them, with Kevin standing outside one with the back door open.

Lester rushed her forward and assisted her into the truck. He slammed the door behind her, shutting her away from the media. It would be a few more minutes until they left. Demi was sure Jaimie was getting Hakim settled in the other truck since he was heading back to their home.

Moments later, Jaimie entered through the other door and sat in the back with her.

"Why are there so many people here?" Jaimie asked.

"I don't know, but this is way more than normal."

"I don't like this. I'm calling Rowan to see if he knows what's going on." Jaimie dug through her bag and pulled out her phone.

Demi stared out the dark tinted windows at the people trying to get a picture of her.

While Jaimie made her call, Demi snuck her phone from her purse. She shot a quick text to Carson to let him know she'd landed in LA.

The front doors opened with Kevin climbing into the driver's seat and Lester in the passenger.

"You ladies okay?" Lester asked, his voice gruff.

He was pissed.

"We're good. Thanks, Lester." She patted him on the shoulder.

"Security around this place is shitty," Kevin muttered. He guided the truck out into traffic.

"What do you mean it's leaked she may not be re-signing?" Jaimie shrieked.

Demi rolled her eyes and leaned back against the headrest. That explained why there was so many paparazzi waiting for her. She was sure the gossip mills were going crazy.

Demi waited patiently for Jaimie.

"Well, that's your job, Rowan," Jaimie snapped. She was completely in her manager role. "Nothing happened in Colorado. She was having fun and relaxing. Demi deserves that."

Demi nodded in agreement.

"What is wrong now?" Demi asked.

"Hold on, Rowan. Let me put you on speaker-phone." Jaimie took her earphones out of her ears and held her phone up. "Go ahead and say again what you just said to me. Demi's with me."

"Hey, Demi girl," Rowan's voice came on.

Demi knew this tone in his voice.

Something was wrong.

"Spit it out, Rowan," Demi said. Her phone in her hand vibrated, signaling a text. Her heart skipped a beat. She slid her finger across the glass screen to open it.

Carson's reply. *I'm glad you made it safe.*

She sent off a quick reply. *I'm missing you already.*

"The media is loving all of the videos that are popping up on social media from Demi singing at the bar," Rowan said.

"It was a karaoke bar!" Demi sniped. One of the frustrating parts of being a celebrity was that no one expected her to do normal things. Who didn't love to go have fun at a bar with friends, alcohol, and singing bad?

"The singing was just a highlight. What's been shared all over the place is that hunk of a man you were oh so cozy with." Rowan's words made her pause.

She hadn't thought about Carson and people trying to figure out who he was.

"Everyone is dying to know who he is."

Her phone buzzed again.

Carson. *Not as much as I miss you.*

Her heart melted. How could she stay away from him too long? Determination filled her. She'd take care of what she was here for then get back on the plane to go to Shady Springs.

"Well, can't you think of something to say?" Demi asked.

"What do you want me to say? Of course I can make things up, but I'm not sure you would want me to just wing it."

Demi glanced at Jaimie whose perfectly sculpted eyebrows were raised.

No, she didn't want him to just wing it.

Rowan could go a little over the top. He had the gift of gab and would weave an elaborate story if they left it up to him.

"I don't want anyone to know about him. If no one has figured it out yet, then leave it. He can just be a mystery man." Demi fidget in her seat. She hadn't spoken with Carson about this type of situation. He was unfamiliar with this sort of limelight. Once the media got their hooks into someone, everyone would know their business.

"If that's how you want to spin it." Rowan sighed.

"I haven't spoken to him about this," Demi admitted. "Let me just speak with him and see if he wants his name out there with mine."

"Why wouldn't he?" Rowan scoffed.

"Not everyone wants to be in the spotlight, Rowan." Demi chuckled.

"Fine. He wants to remain anonymous, then that would build more interest in your lover if no one knows who he is." Rowan added a dramatic flair to his words.

"Just go with that," Jaimie said. She shook her head. "There's nothing wrong with people not knowing who Demi is seeing. There are plenty of celebrities who date normal people not in the industry."

"Yes, that is true, but their name is not Demi Day."

"That is true, Rowan. But Demi Day wants her man to be a secret," Demi retorted. She grinned. It felt kind of good to claim Carson. Even if it was just among her team. "He's mine, and I don't want to share him with the world. At least not right now."

"Got it, boss." Rowan gave a dramatic sigh. "He shall remain the man with no name."

Jaimie took her phone back, and the conversation steered toward the press release that would need to be sent out about her decision. If word was already out that she was not re-signing with the label, then they were going to have to act fast.

Demi glanced forward and found Kevin and

Lester engaged in idle chat. She glanced down at her phone and missed Carson desperately.

She didn't have to worry about paparazzi in the middle of nowhere. And by looking out the window, she could see the LA traffic was going to be a pain to get through. It would take them at least an hour to get to the meeting.

Pulling up the notes on her phone, she typed out words. She loved drawing on her life experiences as inspiration for her songs. Her fans thrived off of knowing that she was like them. She laughed, cried, and fell in love.

Her fingers froze.

Fell in love?

She chewed on her lip, unsure if this emotion she had was love.

She missed the feeling of Carson's strong arms surrounding her, his laugh and his kisses.

The words flowed from her. She tapped in on the emotions that were swirling around in her chest.

"I know that look," Jaimie murmured.

Demi peered up from her phone. She hadn't realized Jaimie had ended the call with Rowan.

"What?"

"You have your writing cap on."

"That's why I wanted to get away. The fresh country air has inspired me." She shrugged.

"Sure it did. You sure it wasn't a certain tall, muscular cowboy that you've been hanging out with?" Jaimie asked softly.

There was no reason for her to lie. Demi cared for Carson, and he was a great guy. She was just afraid that once he got a taste of her real life that he may not want anything to do with her.

"Maybe." She glanced at Lester and Kevin, and they were in a heated discussion about the Lakers and the Golden State Warriors.

Basketball.

Demi shook her head with a small smile on her lips. A nuclear bomb could go off and these two wouldn't hear it. They always argued basketball, both diehard fans of the opposing teams.

"I've been writing. A lot since we arrived in Colorado."

"You think you're ready for the studio?" Jaimie asked.

Demi nodded. She already had a few producers in mind who she wanted to work with. All it would take was a phone call, and they would be in the studio waiting for her.

DEMI SAT BACK IN THE WIDE PLUSH CHAIR in the boardroom and listened to the deal that was being presented to her.

Steel City Entertainment had been her home for years, but now it was time she moved on.

Jaimie sat to her right, while Deb sat on her left. They quietly paid attention to what Steel City was offering her.

"We would want the next album to release in three months, and in six months you would start on your world tour," Sean Limon announced. He was the A&R representative for Steel City. He was someone who was assigned to be the liaison between her, the artist, and the record label.

"How long of a tour are you thinking?" Deb asked quietly.

Demi wouldn't have to speak. Her attorney was paid handsomely to do so for her. Demi trusted Deb would be looking out for her best interests, and right now, an album and a world tour all in the manner of six months would be brutal. Not that it couldn't be done, but it would control her life.

"Fifty cities around the world and about twenty dates here in the States." Sean took his seat next to the executive, Bob King, who ran the label. He was a tough older man, who had an ear for music. He was also the one who felt she was making the wrong decisions to try to hop genres.

Per Deb's advice, they would not be rude, and she would listen to the offer they would put on the table.

At the moment, what the label was offering sucked.

Demi kept her face blank as she turned to Mr. King. He was the one who held on to the purse strings.

What they were talking about would control the next two years of her life.

That wasn't what she wanted. What she wanted was to make her own schedule and spend as much time as she wanted getting to know her cowboy.

Carson's sexy grin came to mind, and she had to hold back her own smile.

Just thinking of him brought a smile to her lips and butterflies in her stomach.

"Sign today, and I'll give you a five-million-dollar bonus. Cash," Mr. King boasted. His smile was one that didn't reach his eyes. He was a ruthless busi-nessman. That was how his company had become so successful.

Jaimie stiffened.

With the amount of money they had made off of her, Demi was curious on what they would offer for her royalties.

"Let's get the point of this meeting," Deb said. She removed her glasses and sat them on the table. "I reviewed the contract, and you want Demi to put out four albums in four years and two tours. The amount you are guaranteeing her is a little on the low end."

Demi sat back. Deb had given her the CliffNotes on the contract, and she was slightly offended.

She bit her lip.

The decision to not re-sign was looking better.

At the end of the day, it wasn't about the money. It was about being paid what she was worth. Mr. King wasn't the one spending countless hours working on the albums, choreography, getting on stage in front of screaming fans each night. There were countless nights she was sore all over, her throat hurt, headaches, stress, anxiety. The fear of letting her fans down would try to consume her. The time she spent away from her family was ridiculous. She was so glad Jaimie was her manager.

Mr. King sat in his office, making more money off of her than she did.

This all stopped today.

"It's a fair deal." Mr. King sniffed.

He had an air of arrogance that rubbed Demi the wrong way.

"You offered Damon Jones a better contract than this. He, who hasn't sold as many albums as Demi, hasn't won any awards like Demi, sold out arenas like Demi, gets a contract worth almost double what you are offing Demi, and he had only one tour to do and three albums in five years."

"I don't know how you saw Damon's contract—"

"I have my ways. Now that is an insult to my client who has been very loyal to Steel City Entertainment," Deb said. "I see here in section four, article B, Steel City would retain all rights to Demi Day's masters."

Demi's gaze flew to Mr. King's. Her last contract, she was able to retain the rights to her own masters. That allowed her to control everything about the music, and it was truly her property, not the label's.

Thank goodness Deb was as thorough as she was.

They were trying to get one over on her.

"We're done." Demi pushed back from her chair. So much for her sitting back and listening to all of the offers they would lay on the table.

"What do you mean, we're done?" Bob sputtered.

His eyes narrowed on Demi. It wasn't often that

anyone turned down a deal from Bob King. He was used to getting what he wanted. With the rumors swirling around that she may not re-sign with Steel City, Deb had shared with her that offers from other labels had been pouring into her office.

Serious money was being offered for her, but she had her own plans in place.

Deb and Jaimie rose from their chairs.

"What I'm saying is that I am going to start looking elsewhere." Demi tilted her chin up proudly. Years ago, when she'd first got her start, she might have taken this deal. But now she was not that naïve girl, she was in a better place in her life and she didn't need this crap.

"No one is going to give you a better deal," Bob snapped.

Demi didn't say a word and stalked toward the door. She knew Deb and Jaimie were right behind her. They exited the room and marched down the hall without a word.

Lester was sitting in the lobby on his phone. At the sound of her heels on the marble floor, he glanced up.

"Done already?" He stood from his chair and pocketed his phone.

"Yup." Demi walked past him, not looking back.

She ignored the gazes from the receptionists and people milling around in the offices.

"Demi. Wait!" Sean shouted from behind her.

She spun on her heel and glared at him. "What is it, Sean?"

"Don't leave like this." He stopped in front of her. He held a worried look in his eyes as he stared at her. "Think about the offer. Maybe you and your team need to contemplate it more. Come back and make a counteroffer. Mr. King will at least listen."

"My client will decide if she wants to make a counteroffer," Deb lied and moved closer to Demi. The woman was fierce when it came to protecting her clients. "At the moment, you can go and tell Mr. King he can take that contract and shove it where the sun doesn't shine."

❧ 18 ❦

arson stretched out on the couch, his arms aching. He lifted his beer to his lips and took a long sip. He was dog-tired but was waiting around to see if Demi would call. It had been over twenty-four hours since he'd seen her.

He knew she was crazy busy, but dammit, he wanted to hear her voice.

She'd texted him at least, but there was nothing better than the sound of her voice.

Well, one thing would be better.

Having her here with him.

He turned the television on and flicked the channel. He paused on the football game and put his feet up on the coffee table. This was what he was needing. Something to help him relax and keep his mind off a certain curvy, brown-skinned beauty.

She'll call—

His cell phone's ringer cut through the air. He snatched it up from the couch, disappointment settling in slightly when he saw it was Wade.

"Yo," he answered. His older brother had better not be calling with an emergency. He'd already had his shower and his sleeping pants on. There was no way in hell he'd be leaving his house tonight.

"Hey, I can't believe I'm doing this," Wade muttered. Joy's muffled voice could be heard in the background. "Joy told me to give you a call."

"What's going on?" Carson was curious. What were they doing, and why would Joy be telling Wade to call him?

"Joy was watching television, and she wants you to turn to that gossip show, *The Hot List* that she watches. They're talking about your girl."

"What channel?" Carson asked. He didn't watch those gossip shows. Hell, if it wasn't sports related, or the news so he could see what the weather was going be, then he didn't bother with it.

Wade's voice grew muffled before he returned, sharing what Joy had told him.

"That's all I wanted. I'll see you in the morning."

"Yup." Carson disconnected the call and surfed the channels until he found the one the show was on.

"Nina Hunt's protégé, Demi Day, is back in LA," the first female correspondent announced. "Word on the street is that she is not happy with her record label and wants out."

"Well, Renee, with Nina on her side, I'm sure Demi will get anything she wants," a black male host said. "Nina has been helping her along the way. Demi would be stupid to not follow the advice of music royalty. Anything Nina touches turns to gold."

They cut to video of Demi being escorted through a mob at the airport. Her head was kept down, and Lester had his arm around her. Her name was shouted over and over as people were vying for her attention.

Carson's pulse pounded in his chest. He finished off the beer and sat the empty bottle down on the table. He was glad Lester was there with her. There was no way she would have been able to navigate through that swarm of bodies.

Whoever was filming followed them out of the airport and outside where she was put into a dark SUV.

"KC, let's be honest, Demi is taking the world by

storm," Renee said when the camera landed on her. "She's about to go into the studio and work on her next album. She's going to have her picking and choosing of labels. They are going to be throwing a ridiculous amount of money at her to sign."

"That's true. She has the world at her feet. Her cosmetic line deal is going to net her at least a half a billion dollars." KC shook his head. "Adore Me wants Demi bad and will pay what they must to get her."

Half a billion dollars?

Carson's heart stuttered.

For makeup?

"Demi Day is a powerhouse and making major moves," Renee said. She grinned, looking into the camera. "The sky is the limit for her. There's no stopping her."

Carson hit the 'off' button on the remote. He felt slightly sick to his stomach. He lost track of time of how long he sat on the couch staring at the blank television screen.

He'd asked her to come back to him.

How could he be selfish and want her back here in Shady Springs? She had so much going for her.

Who was he to get in the way?

He pushed up off the couch and snagged his empty beer bottle. He took it into the kitchen and threw it away, then headed into his bedroom. He wasn't going to think crazy thoughts.

He would wait for Demi to call him. As much he wanted her by his side, maybe that wasn't what was best for her.

He stripped off his clothes and settled into his bed, staring at the ceiling. Blowing out a deep breath, he came to the realization:

She could have it all.

Who was he to make a decision without her? She was a smart cookie. If he'd learned anything about watching his brothers with their women, it was that they worked together. There was no way Maddy would let Parker make a decision for her.

Neither would Joy in anything with Wade. There would be a nuclear war on the ranch if Wade tried something like that.

Carson would show Demi that she could have both worlds.

She was amazing on the stage, yet she yearned for something more. He'd seen it in her eyes when she'd sung at the reception and at the bar.

He could give her what she'd been searching for.

He rolled over to his side, and a smile formed on his lips. His girl didn't know what he had in store for her. He wasn't going to just let her go.

Hell no.

What the hell was he thinking? Why was he doubting himself?

Demi belonged to him, and he was going to prove it to her.

A yawn overtook him. Just as he closed his eyes, his phone rang. He reached for it and saw that it was Demi.

"Hello?" Carson cleared his throat. Suddenly he was no longer tired.

"Hey, there." Demi's smooth husky voice came on the line.

"My superstar," he breathed. Carson fixed his pillows, tucking them underneath his head in a better position. He closed his eyes and allowed the lilt of her voice to wash over him. "You're sounding a little hoarse."

"I know. I went to the studio and I'm paying for it now." She chuckled.

"Recording something new?" he asked. This was a world he was unfamiliar with, but he was willing to learn. Anything that was a part of Demi, he wanted to understand.

"Yeah, it was. I figured since I was in town, I might as well get some things done."

"I'd love to hear you sing for me."

A quick intake of breath was the only noise coming from the phone.

"You want me to sing for you?" she whispered.

"In more ways than one…" He ran a hand along his bare chest and pictured her in his mind.

"You're silly. But I do have a song I wrote that I want you to hear," she admitted.

"I'd love to hear it." He paused, glancing at the empty side of the bed where she would be if she were in town. It was crazy to think that in the short time they had known each other, they had grown so close.

"Yeah? Well, I'll make sure I bring my guitar back with me."

"When will you be back?"

"By the end of the week."

"How'd your meeting go?" Carson didn't want to give away that he was watching a gossip show that had highlighted her. He'd rather hear what was going on with her from the source. Even Carson knew everything on television wasn't true.

"It went to shit quick." She snorted. "I've given my life to that label, and they still shortchange me. I won't be signing with them. What I saw in that meeting just showed that my decision was a sound one. I sort of got pissed off and walked out the meeting. I'm sure that will be on the news by morning."

"Are you okay?"

"I will be once I finish what I need to do here. I have another meeting with Adore Me, and that shouldn't be difficult. I think my lawyers finally reached an agreement with them, so I should be finalizing that soon."

"You are doing amazing things, Demi."

"Awww…thanks. When I get back to you, we will have plenty to celebrate." Demi laughed. It soon faded, and they grew quiet. "I can't wait to see you again."

"Well, you hurry back to me, and we'll have our own private celebration."

"WORD IS OFFICIALLY OUT THAT YOU ARE not signing back with Steel City," Jaimie announced.

They sat at the table in the breakfast nook of her mansion. The last two days had been tiring. Endless meetings with her team had kept her busy.

Demi sipped on her coffee and motioned to the television. "Turn it up."

She normally didn't watch the gossip shows, but

today, she wanted to see what they were saying. Rowan had officially put out a press release while Deb had sent notification to label heads that said she would not be returning.

It was like a weight off her shoulders.

She was free from Steel City.

Her phone had been ringing off the hook. Deb had been wonderful working with Nina's team to configure her own label.

They were still waiting for her to come up with a name. This was one of the hardest decisions she'd had to do. Whatever name she came up with would represent her and her business.

It had to be right.

"Thank you for joining us on the *Hotlist*. I'm Amber Towns." The host smiled into the camera. "There is breaking news today that we are just getting word of. Demi Day has severed ties with her longtime label, Steel City."

"Did you see that coming?" Jamal Brown, the other anchor, chimed in.

Demi had been on their show before as a guest. It was known for their brash reporting on situations in the entertainment business.

"I didn't really think she would go through with it. I was assuming it was a bargaining tactic to get more money or something." Amber shook her head.

Demi snorted. Bargaining tactic? Steel City was getting greedy and played favorites. Demi didn't have time for that. She wanted to do what she wanted, and now she had the capability to do so.

"Now every label is going to be after her. I wonder who she will sign with." Jamal sat back.

They were seated at a wide table across from each other. The *Hotlist* was a popular show that had two different editions. The early morning crew, then the evening crew. Amber and Jamal were much tamer then the others who hosted.

"Word on the street is that Demi is wanting to do country," Amber said.

"What the hell?" Jaimie muttered. She glanced over at Demi who shrugged.

"I haven't exactly hidden that. Anyone would know that." Demi turned back to the television.

"I think she could pull it off. Those Texas roots and that voice. I hope she does it." Jamal chuckled. "She could serenade me anytime singing about cows and dung and I'd be screaming like a crazed fan."

Demi sipped her coffee, hiding her smile. Jaimie tossed her balled-up napkin at her, snorting.

"See, and you were worried. You know there are

plenty of people who are going to be buying this album," Jaimie said.

"Well, she snuck away from LA and is spending some time out in the country. There's been plenty of video that she's found a cowboy to occupy her time." Amber snickered.

"You trying to tell me that I missed the chance to shoot my shot?" Jamal groaned.

"You never had a chance." Amber cackled. She focused on another camera. "Here's Demi living her best life in Colorado while on vacation."

The screen filled with grainy clips of her in the bar with Carson. Video of her singing on stage. Someone had recorded the kiss they'd shared in the bar when she'd stood between his legs.

Jaimie turned the channel. Demi turned away from the television, taking the last sip of her coffee. At the moment, she wished Carson's arms were surrounding her. She loved the feeling of his warmth and strength.

She had to wrap up business, then she'd get back to Colorado.

"Doing this album wasn't for anyone else but for me," Demi admitted. She exhaled and stared down at the table.

"What's wrong?"

Demi looked up and blinked back a few tears. There was so much going on in her life right now that she instantly got choked up.

These weren't sad tears but happy ones.

"I thought my dream had come true when I released my first album," she started. She brushed away one lone tear that trailed along her cheek. She barked a laugh then sniffed. "But this, this is how I know I've made it. I'm no longer tied to any label and make all my own decisions. This is truly making it."

"Oh, sis." Jaimie jumped up and rushed around the table. She threw her arms around Demi and squeezed her tight.

The waterworks flowed from Demi's eyes. She leaned into her elder sister, thankful she had her by her side.

"You deserve all of this. No one has worked harder at this than you."

"Thank you for being here with me." Demi wanted to ensure her sister knew she was appreciated.

"I should be the one thanking you." Jaimie cupped her face, leaning in to plant a kiss on her forehead. "You've taken care of me and Hakim. You have a big heart and didn't have to make sure I had a job where I can still be a full-time parent to my son."

Demi wiped her face and inhaled.

The name of her newly formed company came to her.

"Day Dreaming Music." She watched Jaimie. "What do you think?"

"It's you," Jaimie breathed. "I think it's perfect. Want me to call Deb and let her know?"

Demi nodded and stood from her seat, sliding her cell phone into her back jean pocket. While Jaimie put on her manager hat, Demi had an early morning session with one of her producers. They had already started working on her album.

She was nervous because crossing over was hard to do. Some of her fans may not feel her new music, others would follow her just because.

The real question was if diehard country fans accepted her?

She grabbed a bottle of water from the fridge and made her way through her large home. It was nice and a luxury to have, but she hated the city. She lived in a suburb of LA, and it was considered exclusive, but it wasn't what she really wanted.

An open range and big open sky with a certain cowboy came to mind.

Her phone vibrated.

She pulled it out and didn't recognize the number. Her finger hovered over the 'decline' button, before hitting 'accept.'

"Hello?" She stood at the top of the stairs that led to the lower level of her house where her private studio was located.

"Demi?" a deep baritone voice with a thick Southern accent came through.

"Yes, this is she."

"Hey, girl. It's Chad."

"Chad?" She immediately tried to figure out whose melodious voice was on the other end of the phone.

"Chad Tate." He chuckled.

"Oh, Chad!" She laughed, relaxing. Had it been media or someone from Steel City, she would have hung up. She wasn't sure how Chad got her number or what he was calling for, but she was curious as hell. "I'm sorry. My phone had been ringing off the hook, and I almost didn't answer."

She had met Chad on a couple of occasions at award shows. They didn't run in the same crowd, but they'd spoken a few times. Chad was one of the biggest country stars out. He sold out stadiums everywhere. Just last year, he'd won Male Vocalist of the Year at the Country Music Awards and took home an additional five awards.

"I'm sure it's been crazy. Everyone heard about what happened with you and the label," he said, his voice growing serious. "But that's not what I'm calling about."

"Oh?" She started down the stairway. The members of her recording team would be showing up soon, and she wanted to work on one of the songs she had been writing. She wanted to record it today and to go over the lyrics one more time. Something felt as if it were missing.

"Remember when we were at the Grammys and I suggested we should do a song together?"

Demi almost missed a stair and caught herself from falling down them.

Did she hear him right?

"Yeah, I remember." They had both had a few drinks and were at the same afterparty last year. Chad had come over to the bar where she had been waiting on a drink, and they had struck up a friendly conversation.

"Well, I was completely serious. My sister showed me the videos of you singing in that bar and, girl, I knew you were from Texas, but damn!"

She barked a laugh and continued down to the

lower level, which was completely designed for her music. The lounge area had plenty of space with couches and oversized chairs for people to relax, a full restroom, a guest room, a bar, and then where the magic happened.

Her gaze landed on the doorway that led to the state-of-the-art studio she had installed.

"Why, thank you."

"We can do an even deal. Two songs. One for your album, one for mine," he suggested.

Demi was in shock. Chad Tate was asking her to sing with him. This was unbelievable. Her grin was permanently etched on her face.

"We can work out all the other details later," he said, "but I think we would be good together."

"It's a deal." She didn't need any more convincing. She would be a fool to turn down singing with Chad.

"Well, when you get settled, either you can come on down to Georgia or I'll come to you."

With promises to chat later, Demi disconnected the call and danced in place. Happiness filled her, and if she wasn't careful, she'd combust.

Everything was happening just as she wanted.

Now all she had to do was finish sealing the deal

with Adore Me, then she was going back to Colorado to claim her man.

❦ 19 ❧

"This deal will be a landmark," Betsy Richards announced. The senior vice president of product development for Adore Me cosmetics turned and held her hand out to Demi. "Partner."

Demi took the woman's hand with a wide grin.

Day Beauty would be officially working in partnership with the cosmetic conglomerate. It didn't take much convincing for Adore Me to back Demi and her brand. With Demi's popularity and the influence she had, it was a no-brainer for Adore Me to go into business with her.

Demi had a credible face for the industry. She'd never had cosmetic surgery and was a natural beauty.

Demi's lawyers were agreeable to the contracts and deals. Everything was fair for both sides, which was rare in any big venture.

The industry giant would ensure she had all the tools she would need to succeed.

Demi glanced around the crowded boardroom, and her gaze met Jaimie's. This was a dream of theirs since they were little girls playing in their mother's makeup.

Demi couldn't wait to launch her line. She had so much planned, and the fact that her line would be focused on women of color made it even better. Her mother would be involved in this business venture as well.

A server came around with a tray of champagne. Demi and Betsy snagged one, as did everyone else in the room.

Demi tipped her glass to her team. Jaimie, Deb, Rowan, and Lester were all present with her on this exciting day. They each returned the gesture with wide smiles on their faces.

"Day Beauty." Betsy raised her glass in a toast.

"Day Beauty," echoed back.

Demi took a sip of her champagne and moved over toward her team. She nodded and smiled to the Adore Me executives. This was going to be a great venture for not only her, but their company as well. Adore Me was a company she had had respect for. Their clientele was very diverse, and that made her extremely comfortable working with them.

"This is monumental," Jaimie murmured. She grinned and gave Demi a one-armed hug.

"I know. I just wished Mom would have been here." Demi sighed. Her mother was very stubborn. She didn't want to have anything to do with the 'suits' as she would say. She wanted to be in the lab working on developing products.

"Well, you know her. She would rather have you in the limelight than her." Jaimie patted her on the back.

"Darling, look at you," Rowan exclaimed, stopping next to her. He brushed imaginary lint off her shoulder. "That outfit is to die for."

Demi grinned. She had gone all out for the meeting. She was dressed in a double-breasted Balenciaga sophisticated wool dress. It was low-cut, highlighting her ample cleavage, and it tapered at her waist, putting her hourglass figure on display, stopping mid-thigh. It reminded her of a long suit jacket, and she loved the uniqueness of the outfit. She'd paired it with high-heeled black ankle boots.

Her jewelry was kept simple, makeup light, and her hair was styled in an updo.

There was going to be a press release after this meeting, and she wanted to ensure she dressed her best. For a woman who was completely going into business for herself, she wanted to impress.

"You look dashing yourself." She winked at Rowan.

He was a man of expensive tastes and was always ahead of the fashion world. His deep-mocha skin was smooth and silky, and his locks were pulled back at the nape of his neck. His dark suit was tailored to fit him perfectly as if he was the star.

"Oh, you know how I do." He gave a snap of his fingers. He leaned his glass toward hers.

They clinked them together, laughing.

She sipped the bubbly liquid, taking in the room. Everyone was here because of her. Demi wished Carson could have been here with her. He'd be right by her side, with his arm around her, lending his support.

She missed that man.

Tomorrow she'd be free and clear to fly back to Colorado. She couldn't wait to be in his arms again.

"Demi." Lester's hand rested on her arm.

Demi jumped at the slight touch. She blinked and found him staring at her.

"I'm sorry, what did you say?" She must have zoned out, lost in her thoughts of Carson.

"I said they are ready for the press conference," Lester repeated. He tilted his head to the side, concern on his face. "Are you okay?"

"I'm fine." She gave a forced chuckle. She held up the champagne. "This must be going to my head."

"Follow me." Lester motioned toward the door.

It was then she saw the room had thinned out.

Demi tossed back the rest of the drink and sat the empty glass on the tray of a passing server. Lester led her down the hall to an open room where the media had gathered. It was packed full of reporters ready to get this latest news of her business ventures. Cameramen stood at the back with their equipment focused on the front. Even the local news outlets were here.

It was going to be official.

Day Beauty was going to be a household name.

"And here she is." Mark Nolan, the marketing director for Adore Me, stood at the podium. He motioned for her to join him. The wall behind him was littered with Day Beauty's logo.

Every eye in the room turned to her. Flashes

filled the room as she walked toward the front. Demi smiled and waved at the media. She made it up to Mark who nodded and went over to stand by Betsy and the other executives from Adore Me.

"Hello, everyone. Thank you for joining us on this monumental day," Demi began. She met the gazes of the men and women and smiled. "When I was little girl, my mother worked at a makeup counter at one of the department stores in Waco, Texas."

Demi went over the history of how she'd become infatuated with makeup and healthy skin. Because of her mother, this love was born at an early age. She knew from a young girl that she wanted to own a cosmetic business.

"Day Beauty will not only offer cosmetics and perfumes, we will offer medicated and non-medicated skincare, soap, body care, and personal care products," Demi announced.

A hand rose in the front. A female reporter stared at her with doubt on her face.

"Yes?" Demi nodded to her.

"There has been a slew of celebrities coming out with beauty care products left and right. What is going to make yours so different?" the woman asked.

"I'm glad you asked," Demi admitted. This was

something she had planned to discuss, but this woman had given her an opening. She understood many celebrities or reality television stars had their beauty lines out, but Demi was proud that hers was different. Hers stood out because it catered to people of color.

Day Beauty was going to corner a market.

CARSON TRIED TO STAY BUSY ON THE RANCH while Demi was gone. He had to in order to keep his mind off Demi. He tried to stay away from the television, but he couldn't help it.

Demi was all over the news about launching her cosmetic company. He couldn't turn the channel without seeing someone mentioning her. She was radiant in her suit dress and heels. He caught part of her press conference and was impressed by the way she commanded the room.

She looked comfortable discussing her company.

Seeing her on television wasn't the same.

He wanted to hold her in his arms and keep her body next to his.

Blowing out a deep breath, he walked out his front door. He held a beer and stepped over to the swing on the porch. He took a seat and raised the bottle to his lips, drinking the cool amber liquid.

The sun was on its way down, and the breeze gently blew. He rested his arm along the back of the swing while staring out onto the yard.

He had never realized how lonely and quiet his land was. It was nice, but he imagined a couple of younger versions of himself running around in the yard. He envisaged going out and tossing the pigskin around like he had done with Tyler.

Demi would be sitting next to him, nursing their youngest.

He could see it as if it were real.

Tires rolling over gravel drew his attention to the road leading to his driveway. He glanced over and made out an SUV.

"Well, who the hell is that?" Carson muttered. He took another sip of the beer, finishing it off. He leaned forward and rested his forearms on his knees, waiting for the truck to get closer.

It pulled up to the drive near the front of his home and parked. The back door opened, and Demi came bounding out of the truck.

Carson grinned and set his empty bottle down on the ground. He jogged down to meet her, holding his arms open.

She slammed into him, her laughter filling the air. She wrapped herself around him. He enclosed her in his embrace, breathing in her scent.

"God, woman. I've missed you," he murmured. He glanced down at her. He cupped her cheeks, taking in her wide grin and big brown eyes. She had been gone less than a week, but it felt as if it had been years.

"Not as much as I missed you," she replied.

No longer able to resist, he lowered his head and captured her lips with his.

The kiss was explosive.

It deepened, and his tongue slipped inside her mouth, stroking her tongue. Demi pressed closer to him, her fingers diving into the hair at the base of his neck.

A cough sounded behind them.

Carson lifted his head and peeked over Demi's.

Lester stood with a sheepish look on his face.

"Lester." Carson cleared his throat.

Demi released him and turned, but Carson didn't take his arms from around her. She leaned into him, laughing.

"Carson." Lester gave a nod. He focused his attention on Demi. "Pick you up in the morning?"

"I'll let you know." Demi moved over to Lester.

It was then Carson noticed the duffle bag in the bodyguard's hand. She took it and skipped back over to Carson who seized the bag from her.

Lester eyed him before walking back to the truck. Carson wasn't sure the bodyguard cared for him, but at the moment, Carson didn't care.

He had his Demi.

"Come on, superstar," Carson murmured. Excitement filled him as he took her hand and towed her behind him up the stairs and into the house. He shut the door behind him, pushing Demi up against the door. The bag fell to the floor, forgotten.

His mouth slammed on hers.

A groan tore from her.

Their hands clawed at their clothing. The pile on the floor grew as each item was removed.

He peeled his mouth from hers, catching sight of her in her black lace bra. A growl rumbled from him. He swooped down and buried his face in the hollow of her neck. His hands slipped around her back and undid the clasps of her bra. He slid the contraption from her shoulders, freeing her beautiful mounds.

His gaze took in her swollen lips, her taut dark nipples, and dropped down to her sexy panties.

She was fucking perfect.

And all his.

"Those need to come off," he rasped.

He skated his hands along her waist, hooking his thumbs behind the edge of the small material. He pushed them down, while she kicked them off. They worked together to remove his jeans.

Now they were both naked.

God, she was beautiful.

Her full breasts, tapered waist, smooth brown skin, all made his desire for her rush to his dick. He couldn't explain this intense need to have her.

His cock throbbed with the need to sink deep into her slick channel.

He bent down and lifted her. Their lips merged together in a deep, passionate kiss. His cock brushed against her slick pussy.

He groaned, lining up the blunt tip of his cock to her opening.

He surged forward. Their simultaneous groan filled the air. Demi's drenched core was made for him, wrapping tightly around his cock.

Carson struggled to drag air into his lungs. They fit perfectly together. He wanted to fuck her until neither of them could move or think.

"Carson," Demi whimpered.

Her arms encircled his neck as she held on. She

threw her head back against the door. He peppered hot kisses along the column of her neck.

He couldn't get enough of her.

His hips moved of their own accord, driving him deeper. Each stroke brought him closer to his orgasm.

He loved being inside her.

Their bodies were in sync with each other. Demi rode him, her legs tightening around his waist. Her nails dug into his shoulders with each thrust.

"Demi," he gasped. His lips brushed along her skin, skating up her jawline and ending at her lips. He took her lips in a kiss that he felt clear down to his soul. "I love you."

Her eyes flew open. She cupped his cheeks and smiled.

"I love you, too, Carson." She crushed her lips back to his.

Elation filled him.

She loved him.

Their movements grew more frantic, almost desperate.

Carson's body trembled. He leaned into her, changing the angle of his thrusts slightly.

Demi's release tore through her. Her arms and legs tensed around him, her cry echoing through the air. Her core clamped down around him, sending him into oblivion.

His climax slammed into him. His muscles stiffened as he poured himself into the woman he loved.

Carson buried his face into her neck again, breathing in her intoxicating scent.

They stilled, Carson holding most of Demi's weight. At the moment, he could barely move. They couldn't stay here. It was time to take this reunion to the bedroom.

Carson slowly withdrew from Demi. He lowered her to the floor, his arms around her. There was no way he was letting her go. She opened her eyes and smiled at him.

"Mr. Brooks, that was one hell of a way to greet me." A scream erupted from her when he swooped down and picked her up in his arms.

He made his way through the house and headed toward his bedroom.

"I'm not done yet, superstar."

‪⁂‬ 20 ‪⁂‬

Demi sat on the back porch of Carson's home with her iPad in her lap. She paused her writing and stared out at Carson who was currently hammering a nail into the bottom step of the porch.

Everything about the man was damn near perfect.

His smile. His eyes.

He was caring. Genuine.

And he loved her.

How did she get so lucky?

The minute she had stepped foot back in Shady Springs, she'd wanted to be in his arms. Lester had insisted on coming back to Colorado with her since word had got out about which town she was staying in. She had kept Carson's identity a secret and prayed that it stayed that way.

She wouldn't wish what she went through on him.

A sigh escaped her.

There wouldn't be any way she would be able to keep him hidden forever.

"Keep staring at me like that and I'm going to think you want something," Carson's deep baritone voice broke through her thoughts.

She blinked and sent him a smile.

They had spent the entire night and half of the morning tangled together in his bed. She was slightly sore from their frantic lovemaking last night.

"I was just thinking." She shrugged.

"Anything I can help with?" He stood to his full height and dropped the hammer into his toolbox sitting on the ground.

"Keep being you."

A lopsided grin spread across his face. He walked up the stairs and came to the top of the landing. He leaned against the pillar and focused his attention on her.

"What are you doing?" He nodded toward her iPad.

"Writing." She held it to her chest. She was shy

when it came to her inner thoughts and feelings. She loved putting them down and bringing them to a song.

"Anything good?" he asked.

"Maybe." It was a warm fall day, and she was enjoying it. This was what she had dreamed about.

Lazy days. Wind blowing in her hair while she relaxed in a chair with her man working in the yard.

She pushed up from her seat and walked over to him. She kept her tablet cradled in her arms and stopped in front of him. She stood on her tiptoes and nuzzled her face into the hollow of his neck, inhaling his scent. She kissed him.

A rumble escaped him.

His arms wrapped around her and pulled her in close.

"Don't try to distract me," he murmured.

Those steel-gray eyes of his darkened. Her breath caught in her throat. One look from this man, and she softened like putty in his hands.

"Is it working?" She grinned.

"A little." He dropped a kiss on her forehead. He cupped her face in his hand, running his thumb down her cheek.

She leaned into his hand, loving the feeling of his callused palm against her smooth skin.

"Are you going to tell me, or do I have to coax it out of you?"

She chuckled and shook her head. "You are so impatient."

"Only when it comes to you."

"Fine." She blew out a deep breath and motioned for him to sit on the stairs. She followed him down and took her spot on the stair below him. She rested back against him, cradled between his thighs. She slid her finger along the screen of her tablet. "Now this is a rough draft, and I will polish it up later."

"You don't have to be nervous around me." He stroked her hair softly, tucking it behind her ear. He leaned down, his lips brushing her ear. "Just read it, baby."

A shiver ran through her spine.

Butterflies fluttered in her stomach. She didn't know why, but she was nervous to read what she had written to Carson. What he thought was impor-tant to her.

Carson's hand slid gently down her back, comforting her. Heart racing, she opened her mouth and let the words flow from her lips.

"I returned to you.

It felt as if I were gone forever.

Standing in front of you felt like home.

My heart was here.

All along I knew, it would be safe with you.

"WHEN YOU'RE LOOKIN' AT ME, WITH THOSE sexy gray eyes.

It takes my breath away.

But here we are, together again.

Saying I love you.

"WRAP ME IN YOUR ARMS.

Don't ever let me go.

I want to spend forever with you.

Every night make me yours."

She stopped singing. Her chest rose and fell swiftly, and her pulse pounded in her ears. This was the most exposed she'd ever felt in her life.

It had been early this morning, when she'd woken up. Carson had still been asleep, his arms wrapped around her. She had snuck from the bed to relieve herself, and when she'd gone back into the room, her eyes had taken him in.

She'd crawled back into the bed and lay on her side watching him sleep.

The words to this song had come to her, and

immediately she'd wrote them. All the while watching him. This was the most at peace she'd felt in a long time. Now that her destiny was in her hands, she could focus on what would make her happy.

Demi opened her eyes and glanced over at Carson who stared at her without saying a word.

"Well?" Demi cleared her throat, unable to read Carson's expression.

"Demi, baby." Carson reached up and moved her hair from her face. His hand skated down to the back of her neck and brought her face close to his. He brushed his lips against hers. "That was amazing. I don't know what to say, except to say you've left me speechless, which doesn't happen often."

"It's how I feel," she admitted bashfully.

"How do you come up with words like that?" His gray eyes watched her. His hands rested on her waist, holding her close to him.

She shrugged, admitting what inspired her to write it.

"Woman, you are amazing." He teased her lips with his again when she was done with her recount of that morning.

Demi groaned, moving her lips to his. She needed more of him.

They were interrupted by the shrill sound of her phone ringing. She recognized the tone.

It was Jaimie.

"I have to get that," she murmured. Demi stood and jogged up the stairs and snagged her phone from the table near the chair she had been sitting in. "Hello?"

"It's official!" Jaimie practically hollered into the phone.

"What?" Demi laughed at her sister's enthusiasm.

"Day Dreaming Music is official!" her sister announced. "The trademark was accepted, and Deb has worked her mojo. Your record label is now ready for business."

"Are you kidding me?" Demi danced in place.

Deb was worth every penny. The woman could work miracles, and this was proof of it.

"No, so we need to get you back into the studio. We need to sit down and talk things through. Album, marketing, tours."

"You have been busy," Demi said.

Carson came up behind her and wrapped his arms around her waist. She leaned back into him, loving his warm embrace.

"That's why you pay me so well. I have everything lined up for the studio, and with as much as you've been writing, we can have this album done in a month if we really push hard."

"But wait. You said tour?" Demi glanced up at Carson.

He watched her quietly. Worry filled her. She wasn't sure if she was ready to go out on tour. She'd just turned down a contract that would have had her out on the road for a year and a half.

Now Jaimie wanted her off gallivanting cross the world?

"Yes, ma'am. Did you forget that's where the big money is? We will need to be on the road to push the album. You're crossing genres, and we are going to have to introduce you to a new world of fans."

Jaimie was right.

"Sounds like we will be heading back to LA soon," she murmured, disappointment filling her.

"I have studio time and everyone set for next week." Jaimie released a sigh. "I know you were wanting to stay here in Shady Springs longer, but right now, we have to get back to LA. There aren't any studios here, and it would take too long to outfit one here."

"Fine. We'll go back."

"Also one other thing." Jaimie paused dramatically.

"What is it?" Demi grew suspicious when her sister did this. She never knew what to expect.

"The Writers' Guild has invited you to be a presenter at the awards," Jaimie shrieked.

Demi rolled her eyes, a smile forming on her lips. The Writers' Guild was the industry award dinner that was a big deal. It was a formal dinner and award ceremony of peers. It was a red-carpet event and was covered heavily by the media. Demi had been nominated a few times but had yet to win an award.

"You have to accept," Jaimie said.

"I'm not going to pass the opportunity up." She would be a fool to not go. Demi always had fun when she attended, and it allowed her to network amongst her peers.

"Good. I'll go ahead and let them know that you will be there," Jaimie replied. "We're only going to have another day or two here. Let me know when I need to book our flight back to LA."

"Okay, okay." Demi spun around in Carson's arms and leaned her forehead against his chest. "I'll call you back."

"You do that. I hope you and the boyfriend have come up for air."

"None of your business. Bye." She disconnected the call before her sister could come back with something smart to say.

"Sounds like you will be heading out back to California before you were ready." He slid a comforting hand down her back.

She nodded without saying a word. She choked up and didn't want to start crying in front of him. She had to be strong, weakness wasn't going to be an option. There were so many people depending on her, and she couldn't let them down.

Sighing, she gave him a half-hearted smile.

"Want to come to Cali with me?" Demi bit her lip, unsure of his response. It wouldn't be long, and she wanted him to experience her world. If he wanted to get to know the real Demi Day, then he would have to come visit her in her element. Taking him to her home and to the event would be fun.

"You want me with you?" he asked, raising an eyebrow.

"Of course I do." She slid a hand up his chest and cupped his cheek. "You don't happen to have a tuxedo lying around, do you?"

"Look at our little brother. Jet-setting off to California to be arm candy." Wade cackled. He brought a long-neck bottle up to his lips and took a swallow.

"Wow. Hollywood. Who would have thought Carson would be involved with a major superstar?" Parker laughed, hitting his knee. "Are you gonna wear those big black sunglasses that all the stars wear?"

He and Wade burst out in a fit of laughter.

Carson grinned, enjoying Parker and Wade busting his balls. It was the end of the day, and they were just hanging out by the barn like they used to do when they were teenagers. There was nothing better than chilling with his siblings after a long hard day. Carson enjoyed the time he got to spend with them.

"A man who looks this good don't need to hide behind shades." Carson scrubbed a hand along his jawline.

They burst out laughing again. It was no secret that the Brooks men were handsome. They had taken advantage of their looks their entire lives. Ladies had flocked to them, and they had never been short on willing women to warm their beds.

Now, life was different.

"Well, we are exclusive now," he admitted. It had been a while since Carson had considered himself a one-woman man. Not that he was the cheating type, but he liked to have options. Now the only person he wanted in his life was Demi. There would be no other for him.

"You don't think this is too fast?" Wade asked. He raised an eyebrow at Carson.

"We aren't getting married." Carson scoffed. "She wants me to visit her home there and be her date to some fancy dinner."

He was a little nervous at the fact that he would be around celebrities and such. He may have gone off to college and played football, but this was nothing compared to Demi's life.

He was a country boy at heart. What did he know about the music industry, or Hollywood and red-carpet events?

"Well, she seems to be down to earth," Parker said. "Now don't go trotting off to California and come back thinking you are too good to work this ranch."

His brother nudged him with his elbow. Carson shook his head, knowing they were going to be ribbing for months to come.

"Don't worry. I won't forget how to cover for you

two when you're slacking around this place." Carson jumped up, avoiding Parker's hands.

"Don't think I can't whip your ass, boy," Parker threatened, pointing his beer at him.

"Those are fighting words." Wade chuckled.

Carson laughed, brushing dirt off his jeans. He loved Parker and Wade and he would miss them. He wasn't planning to be gone long. Parker and Wade would take care of his responsibilities for him. He would be gone no more than a week and a half.

"So I take it y'all are getting serious?" Parker asked, settling down. He leaned back against the fence and readjusted his hat on his head.

Carson exhaled, walking back over to his spot and sat in between Parker and Wade. Were they getting serious?

Hell yeah.

"Yup. We've even said the L word," he admitted.

Wade let out a low whistle. "Already?"

"When you know, you know," Carson said.

"I'll drink to that," Parker murmured. "I'm happy for you, little bro."

"Me, too." Wade raised his empty bottle in the air. "Will you look at us. A few years ago, I wouldn't have thought any of us would have settled down. Ma would be so happy."

They grew quiet. Wade was right. Their mother would be ecstatic to know that her boys had found good women and settled down. A gentle breeze blew as if she confirmed she was looking down on them. Carson glanced up and smiled. He sure did miss his mother. It would have been amazing for her to see her boys grow up into the men they had become. He would have loved to have Demi meet her. His mother would have loved her.

"And to think Pa used to ride our asses to get married to 'good girls.'" Parker sighed. He finished off his drink and sat the bottle next to him.

Carson went silent.

Get married?

He wasn't sure he and Demi were there yet. He loved that woman with all of his soul. The song she had written and sung for him resonated deep inside. The way she was able to channel her feelings into words and then to hear the words float from her lips in the most beautiful voice he'd ever heard.

And it was all for him.

"What happened with you and Pa?" Carson asked.

It was something that had been weighing heavy on him. What had gone down between Parker, Maddy, and Jonah was epic. He would never have thought they would have been in a place where they allowed Jonah to be at their wedding.

"Pa showed up to the house and wanted to speak with Maddy and me. He apologized." Parker paused. He removed his hat and pushed a trembling hand through his hair before putting the cap back on. "I've never seen anything like it. Pa teared up and was truly genuine with the apology. It doesn't make up for everything. We both know we had a role to play in what happened between us, but he wanted to make amends for his part."

Carson and Wade remained quiet.

Jonah Brooks going around apologizing was something new. Carson never would have thought he would see the day Jonah admitted he was wrong about anything until he'd confessed his shortfalls to Carson at dinner.

"Well, I'm happy Pa is trying to make amends for everything he's done," Wade said. "Maybe now we can move forward as a family and start creating new memories."

✺ 21 ✺

"Oh my," Demi murmured.

She froze in place, her gaze locked on Carson. He strode out of her walk-in closet, his tuxedo fitting him perfect. Words couldn't express how devilishly handsome her man was.

He was breathtaking in jeans and his plaid shirts, but seeing the cleaned-up Carson, she was left speechless. The tailored suit, clean-cut face, and striking gray eyes had her mesmerized.

This was her man.

They had returned to LA two days ago, and it had been a whirlwind. The second they were back, Demi was being pulled in a thousand different directions. Dress fittings, studio time, meetings about her cosmetic line and record launch. Her days may have been stressful and busy, but the nights were filled with Carson.

The man knew how to help her unwind. He had made love to her each night, leaving her spent and falling asleep in his arms. His strong embrace was comforting and allowed her to get the best sleep she'd had in years.

"Didn't think I knew how to put one of these on, did you?" Carson joked. He modeled his dark suit before striding forward toward her. He swept her up into his arms and pulled her close.

"I may have to find reasons to keep putting you in these." She leaned up and kissed his lips. Even with her heels on, she still had to stretch up to kiss him.

She was nervous about tonight. It would be the first time she'd step out with her new boyfriend. The media was already in a frenzy about her secret man in Colorado.

"Let's not make it too often." He grimaced, reaching down to adjust himself. "And that dress of yours, I don't know if I want everyone seeing my woman's body."

Demi giggled and stepped back from him. She twirled around to show it off. It was a floor-length sleeveless trumpet dress that molded to her curvy figure. There was a high split that showed off her entire leg. She was in love with the color. Janet had chosen a sparkling mint green that looked great against the tone of her skin.

"You don't like it?" She battered her eyelashes at Carson.

A playful growl escaped him.

"I like it too much." He adjusted himself again.

Lord, he shouldn't do that. She knew exactly what was underneath his hands. Her pulse pounded in her ears as the memory of last night came to mind and how hard he'd fucked her.

He tried to grab for her, but she ducked out of the way of his hands. As much as she would love to dive back into her bed with him, Jaimie would have her neck if they were late.

"You sure about going out with me to this event?" She bit her lip, worry filling her. Would this be too much for him? The media were like rabid wolves and would want to know everything about him and plaster it everywhere.

Just because he was with her.

"Baby."

The term of endearment had her melting against him.

He wrapped his arms around her and pulled her

to him. He tipped her chin up, forcing her to meet his gaze. "If you want me there, then I'm there."

"I just want to warn you, people are going to be all over you wanting to know everything about you. My team has been trying to keep you out of the tabloids. Some of the paparazzi may not even be nice about it—"

She remembered what Nina had gone through when she'd started dating Sid. The media had not been nice because not only was she dating a non-celebrity, but he was white. It had been hard on them at first, but Nina had shut all of that down.

"I have big shoulders and can weather anything. Don't worry about me. I'm a big boy and can take care of myself." His gray eyes bored into her.

Their color was so rare and mesmerizing that she would have sworn he could see into her soul.

"I just don't want you getting hurt," she mumbled.

He leaned down and kissed her softly.

"Nothing could hurt worse than a linebacker slamming into you, or getting kicked by a damn bull. If I can live through that, I can make it through men and women with cameras." He grinned.

His head came down again, and this time she sideswiped him.

If she weren't careful, her clothes and his would be on the floor.

"No time for that. We have to go." She walked over and scooped up her tiny clutch and motioned for him to follow her.

"You sure?" He chuckled.

"I'm very sure." She turned back to him and winked.

She took him by the hand, entwining their fingers. They left her master suite and made their way through the house.

Everyone was waiting for them down in the family room.

"Wow. You two make one hell of a couple," Jaimie breathed. She stood from her perch on the couch.

Lester and Janet were waiting also.

"Why is your lipstick messed up?" Janet's eyes narrowed on Demi. She rested her hands on her waist and glared at Carson.

"She kissed me." Carson shrugged nonchalantly.

"Really?" Demi's gaze flew to him. Talk about getting thrown under the bus.

He chuckled and strode over to the bar and poured himself a small glass of bourbon.

"Come here." Janet waved her over to the table

where her mini kit was. "What am I going to do with you two?"

Demi tried to keep from smiling, but she was fighting a losing battle. She was in love and couldn't help that she couldn't stop kissing Carson.

Janet fawned over her. She made little *tsk* noises as she fixed her makeup.

"So we need to go over point of entry to the event," Lester began.

Demi half listened to her security lead. He always took his job seriously, and she knew without asking that it would be more than just him at the event.

"Point of entry?" Carson's eyebrows rose high. "Sounds like we are infiltrating the Pentagon or something."

"Don't get him started." Demi groaned.

"Oh boy," Janet muttered. She touched a brush to Demi's lips.

"No, we are not infiltrating, but we have to plan out a strategy to get Demi in safely and out unharmed."

The room grew silent. Demi glanced back over to Carson who sat his drink down. A scowl formed on his face.

"Has someone tried to harm her?" he asked quietly.

"There have been some altercations of fans going too far. I'm just going to leave it at that. Once Demi is inside, we will be good to go. Kevin and I will be inside. You won't see us."

Janet pulled out her other brushes and fiddled with her makeup. Demi's gaze connected with Carson's. She could see he didn't like that she could be in danger, but unfortunately, it came with the job.

"Nothing big has ever happened. Lester and his team are always there," Demi said, hopefully defusing the situation.

Lester continued on, giving Carson instructions on what to do, where to stand. They were going to try to keep the media off of him as much as possible, but once his name leaked out, there was no turning back.

"I'll be fine." Carson came over to stand by her side just as Janet stepped back.

"There. Perfect." She teased Demi's hair to make sure not a strand was out of place. "Done."

"All right. Let's get ready to roll out," Lester announced.

Everyone in the room scurried around to prepare to leave.

"Beautiful." Carson took Demi's hand and brought it to his lips. He studied her for a moment.

"Don't worry, baby. I'll be at your side the entire time."

"You better be." Demi grinned.

"With this dress on, baby. I'll be stuck to your side like glue."

THE DOOR TO THE OVERSIZED SUV OPENED. Carson stepped out first, squinting at the flashes from the cameras.

Holy hell.

He turned back and held out his hand for Demi. She placed her smaller one in his and allowed him to help her from the truck.

Her named was screamed by crazed fans. He held back a grin. He didn't mind being eye candy tonight. This was something for her line of work, and he wanted to be there for her. It was actually pretty cool.

This little country boy was in Hollywood on the arm of a famous celebrity.

His woman.

Demi stood near him. Her dress flowing around her ankles and was downright sexy.

There was no one else who could hold a candle to

his woman tonight. Her curves were highlighted by the mint-green dress.

He had been aroused since the moment he had awoken. Demi done up in her makeup and fancy dress had him tongue-tied, but nothing compared to her in jeans, a t-shirt, and her clean, makeup-free face.

His girl had something most of these people in Hollywood didn't have.

Natural beauty.

"This is insane," he murmured, bringing her close to him. With seeing the chaos, he was glad Lester had gone over what to expect. He'd watched a few award shows in his life, but that didn't do anything to prepare him for the real-life situation. There were camera crews everywhere, people screaming and shouting.

"I told you." Demi smiled.

They walked along the red carpet as he had been instructed by Lester. It didn't sit well with him that she had to have a security team to ensure fans wouldn't go too far. But whatever he had to do to keep safe, he would.

"Demi! Over here," a woman shouted. She waved for Demi to come over to her.

"And now it begins." Demi squeezed his arm. She led them over to the reporter.

The woman was in a white dress, and her blonde hair was pulled back in a complicated bun.

"Here we have Demi Day," the woman announced, looking over into the camera. Her eyes didn't miss a beat and narrowed in on Carson.

"Karen, how are you?" Demi asked.

They shared a small hug. Demi turned on her mega-watt smile as she focused on the reporter. She stepped away and slid her hand back into his.

"I'm doing well. Who are you wearing tonight?" Karen asked.

"Gaston Noir." Demi stepped back, releasing his hand so she could model the dress.

Carson held in a growl. Deep down, he didn't want anyone appreciating the curves Demi had on display.

"That is a fabulous dress. And who do we have with you?" Karen's focus returned to him.

Demi and her team had prepped him as well as they could, but he wasn't worried. He wanted the world to know Demi was taken.

Demi glanced at him briefly. He held his hand out to her to draw her to him. He brought her in close and faced Karen.

"This here is my boyfriend," Demi murmured, turning her warm brown eyes on him.

His heart skipped a beat at the title bestowed upon him.

"Carson Brooks." He held out his hand to Karen who took it immediately in a firm grip.

"Well, nice to meet you, Carson. It's so good to speak the man who has had the media in a frenzy."

Carson grinned. From what Demi had tried to tell him, the media would want to know everything about him. There wasn't anything about his past that he was ashamed of. They could dig all they wanted, but they would be disappointed.

"There's nothing special about me. I'm just a rancher from Colorado." He chuckled.

"There must be something special about you to keep Demi out in the country." Karen laughed. She swiveled her attention to Demi. "Are you presenting an award tonight?"

"Yes, I am." Demi went on about her presentation.

Carson's eyes were drawn to the massive amount of people surrounding the carpet trying to get all of the stars' attention. He caught sight of Lester, who as promised, remained in the background. The security guard's focus was on them and the area.

His gaze landed on someone he did recognize.

Chad Tate.

Carson was a huge fan of the country singer.

At the moment, the singer had caught sight of Demi and was headed their way.

"Thanks so much." Demi took his hand and pulled him away from the reporter. "That wasn't so bad."

"Demi!" a deep baritone voice called out.

She spun around, a grin spreading on her face.

"Chad!" she squealed. She let go of Carson and dashed toward Chad who hugged her. Chad Tate was tall and fit with dirty-blond hair cut close to his head. He was considered a sex symbol by the women, and the longer Carson looked at him, the more he realized they were alike.

Jealously instantly reared its ugly green head.

Not that Carson had any worry about Demi being unfaithful.

He just didn't appreciate another man putting his hands on his woman.

"Carson." Demi waved him over to them.

He arrived, keeping a smile on his face, not wanting to share his displeasure.

"Chad, this is my boyfriend, Carson Brooks. Carson, this is—"

"Chad Tate. Huge fan." Carson grinned, holding out his hand.

Chad took it in a firm grip, returning the smile.

"Thanks, man. Appreciate it," Chad said. He glanced back at Demi. "You just let me know where we're going to meet up at, and I'm there."

"I will." Demi smiled.

She leaned into Carson, and he would have to admit it did something for him to have her always touching him. He wrapped an arm around her waist.

Chad gave a nod to Carson and moved on.

"What was that all about?" Carson murmured, his lips brushing the top of Demi's head.

"Chad called me and offered to do a song with me." Demi's smile grew wider.

"Really? That's awesome." Carson was proud of Demi. She wanted to sing country, then there was no better person for her to work with than Chad.

They continued on with Demi stopping for a few more reporters. She had a way about her that left all of the people interviewing her smiling. Everyone was curious about him, and Carson didn't have any issues standing by Demi's side.

She was a star and was shining bright.

Demi had even stopped and posed for selfies with

the fans who were lined up along the fence to keep the general public at bay.

When speaking with the media, she deflected questions she didn't want to answer, was professional, and kept him close to her.

"I'm done with questions." Demi laughed.

"All right. Let's go inside." Carson took her hand and led her into the building. It was hard for him not to be star struck. There were a lot of industry people there that he recognized from television on the rare occasion he watched.

Once they were in the building, they were escorted to their table. He assisted Demi with her chair before taking the one beside her.

"You doing all right?" she asked, eyeing him.

"I should be asking you that." He chuckled. He scooted his chair closer and rested his arm along the back of hers. "Everyone wants your attention. I'm good with being in the background."

The room was decked out in expensive decorations. The tables were round and covered with white cloths. They were set for six people. He was curious who would be sitting with them.

Crystal chandeliers hung over them, casting a soft light around them. The room could almost be described as magical. Flowers adorned the centerpieces.

"Look who it is," a husky voice said.

Carson turned and saw a handsome couple stopping at their table.

"Nina!" Demi stood and rushed around and hugged the other woman.

She looked familiar to Carson, but he wouldn't have known who she was.

"Sid, how are you?" Demi asked.

"We are doing well." The woman's husband was tall and buff. He appeared about as uncomfortable in his penguin suit as Carson was.

Carson stood from his seat and went over to them.

"Nina and Sid, this is Carson—"

"The mysterious guy from Colorado." Nina smiled.

Carson shook her and Sid's hand.

"Not sure I was trying to be mysterious." Carson grinned.

"Don't let the girls tease you so. It wasn't too long ago that I was the man no one knew." Sid laughed.

Carson instantly felt a connection to him. He

appeared to be the type Carson wouldn't have an issue sharing a beer with.

The girls sat, instantly falling into conversation. Carson and Sid continued to stand near them.

"How did you and Demi meet?" Sid asked.

"At a restaurant. She was looking for something to eat, and my brother and I helped her and Jaimie out." Carson shrugged. He had a sense that Sid wasn't in the same industry as their women. "You?"

"Me and Nina met when she came looking for a personal trainer." Sid chuckled. That certainly explained Sid's solid physique. "I've been where you are, and let me give you a little advice."

"I'm all ears." Carson was interested in anything the man had to suggest to him. It was nice to know there was someone who knew what he was going through.

Sid glanced at Nina, turned back to him, then moved closer.

"Let's just say there was a bunch of people who didn't want me and Nina together, just because I was white and she was black."

"What?" Carson's smile faded. Race had never been a factor in Carson's life. He treated all people the same. He thought of his two sisters-in-law, and his nephew.

They were family, and he would never tolerate someone treating them different because of the color of their skin.

In this day and age, race should not be an issue. Not that Carson was ignorant to the world, but he would not go for anyone talking bad about him, Demi, or any member of his family.

"Yeah, and they were not kind to Nina at all." Sid grew serious. "But just remember, it's not anyone's business what goes on between you and Demi."

Carson nodded, thanking him before taking his seat next to Demi.

The noise level in the room grew as more people were seated at their tables. Unable to resist touching her, he took Demi's hand and brought it to his lips.

"Everything okay?" she asked.

He gazed into her big brown eyes and knew he would be ready to defend his relationship with this woman.

He nodded and kissed her forehead.

"Of course." He leaned in to whisper in her ear, "It'll be better once I can peel you out of this dress."

❦ 2 2 ❦

Demi was riding high on the Writers' Guild dinner. She had a ton of fun at the event. Having Nina and Sid sitting at her table made it even more enjoyable. She was happy that Carson and Sid appeared to hit it off. As close as she was with Nina, she'd wanted Carson and Sid to become friends.

Demi presented the award for Favorite Male Artist. This award show differed from the Grammys or American Music Awards because it was peer-driven, not industry-driven where there were certain panels who voted for the winners.

No, this award banquet was voted on by them and made it all the more special.

Of course, Chad had won.

He was hard-working and deserved it.

Now that the show was over, there were plenty of afterparties going on. Demi had planned to go to one. She had received an invite to Austin Keller's. Not only was he one of the most popular country music producers in the business, he had heard of the record she was recording and had reached out to her.

Lester had escorted them home for a quick dress change, then he'd carted them off to Kyle's place that wasn't too far from Demi's.

"This is completely networking," Demi murmured. She held Carson's hand while they were chauffeured to the party.

With these award shows and parties, she could easily stay out until the crack of dawn.

But that wasn't Demi.

She was only attending this one because it was going to be business-related. She wanted to make sure she made all the connections she needed to help her launch her next album. It was important that she gained the support from country's best.

"This should be fun." Carson leaned back against the plush leather seat and stared out the window.

She bit her lip and stared at him. She didn't know what to think of him at the moment.

Was this too much for him?

Were they moving too fast?

She grew worried and didn't want to scare him away. Maybe inviting him to come with her was a bad idea.

He must have felt her eyes on him. He turned around and glanced over at her.

"What's wrong?" he asked softly.

"Nothing." She paused, then let out a sigh. "I'm lying. I'm worried that this may be too much for you."

"I'm fine. It's a lot to take in. I always assumed that rock stars just partied hard and didn't have to do anything else." He squeezed her hand in his. "I'm learning fast that it's a lot of hard work."

"It is. There is only so much my manager and team can do. Eventually people will want to speak with the artist and get a sense of who they are dealing with."

"Makes sense to me. Not too different than the cattle industry. Before we sign on to do business with a company, I like to meet with them and get a sense of the type of people running the business. Our name and quality of cows is important to my family. We can't just be associated with anyone."

"I, for one, am not a person who likes to stay out

all night and party. I'll be making my rotation, stay maybe an hour to be nice, then we can leave."

"Whatever you want. I'm just your hot arm candy," he jested.

"I'm such a lucky girl." She leaned over and offered her lips to him.

He bent down and captured them in a sizzling kiss. An electric current made its way straight to her core.

How could this one man affect her so?

He was the most handsome man at the dinner. Carson drew many eyes his way. Now he was dressed more casual in jeans, a button-down, and a sport coat, he was still smoking-hot.

"If we keep this up, I can't promise I will keep my hands to myself," Carson murmured, his lips brushing hers.

Demi didn't know when her hand had made it between them and grasped his shirt in her fist.

"If this wasn't so important, I may take you up on that." Demi giggled. She glanced toward the partition that separated them and Lester and Kevin in the front of the truck. All they would have to do was slide the tinted glass shut and they would have full privacy.

"Don't tempt me, woman," Carson growled playfully.

He nipped at her ear, sending a shudder through her.

If only…

She shook her head. There would be plenty of time for him to make good on a promise.

The truck slowed and turned onto the long winding driveway.

"We're here," Lester announced.

"Splendid," Demi said. She kissed Carson's cheek.

"What is that for?" he asked.

"Just a promise for later." She winked. This hour that she planned to be at Kyle's party was going to be the longest of her life.

Carson grinned and brought her hand up to his mouth. He dropped a kiss to the back of her hand.

"You remember that, baby."

"I can't forget." She motioned for him to bend down so she could whisper in his ear. She didn't want Lester or Kevin hearing what she had to say. "My panties are soaked."

Carson's head jerked back, and his eyes were wide. He released a curse and glanced down at his watch.

"One hour?" he said.

"One hour."

They pulled up to an ostentatiously large mansion. Lester stopped the truck up in the circled drive that led to the front door. The back door opened with a valet standing beside the car.

"Ms. Day, welcome to Mr. Keller's party." The young man held out his hand and helped her down from the SUV.

Carson exited from the other side and came over to meet her.

Lester would handle the car, and then he and Kevin would enter the home. She knew the routine already.

Carson offered her his arm. She wrapped her hand around him and allowed him to escort her to the front door.

"Look at this house." Carson let loose a low whistle.

"Austin is one of the biggest country music producers and writers. He's worked with every big-named star in country."

"Ah, hence why we are here since you are recording your first country album." Carson brought her in closer to him.

There were lots of people milling around outside.

Security appeared to be tight. She wouldn't expect anything less when parties were thrown at a private residence.

They entered the home, finding the house to be packed. Soft music played in the background, while laughter and chatter filled the air.

"Lead the way," Carson murmured.

Demi nodded, unsure where to start. She glanced around and recognized some faces. She entwined her fingers with Carson's and towed him behind her.

Her second dress of the night was a little black number that stopped mid-thigh. It dipped down in the front to put her ample cleavage on display and had a low backline that went down as far as her waist. Her four-inch sandals completed the look.

They entered the formal living room and began making their way around the room. A server brushed past with a round tray with glasses of wine. She scooped up one and motioned to Carson to see if he wanted one.

"Nah, wine isn't my thing." He shook his head.

"If you are looking for a bar with real alcohol, it's in the room across the hall."

Demi turned around and found herself facing Maddox Vaughn, an up-and-coming country sensation. He took one look at her and squinted.

"You look familiar."

"Hi, I'm Demi—"

"Demi Day." Maddox laughed.

He was a young guy who was crazy with a guitar. Women flocked to him, and Demi was sure within the next year, he'd be giving Chad a run for his money on the charts.

"It took me a second to recognize you. How are you?" he asked.

"I'm doing well." Demi smiled.

"I'm going to head to the bar. You want anything?" Carson asked, his lips brushing her ear.

She shook her head and held up her wine glass. He kissed the top of her head and walked away, leaving her in conversation with Maddox.

"I hear you are coming over to country," Maddox said.

"Sounds like everyone knows before I even made an announcement." Demi laughed.

"You know no one can keep a secret in this industry."

"I guess it isn't a bad secret to let out. It's something I've been wanting to do for a long time," she admitted.

"We need more women singing. The charts are crowded with us men," Maddox said.

"I've noticed that. I wonder why that is," she said.

"Not sure, but we are definitely needing more diversity, too."

Demi's eyebrows shot up in surprise. She took a sip of her wine, not wanting to say something that would offend him.

"I mean no offense," Maddox went on, obviously reading her expression. "I'm actually a big fan of yours. Your album, *All the Way*, was one of my favorites. I kept that on repeat."

"Thank you."

"Are you here to meet with Kyle?" Maddox asked.

"Actually I am. He invited me to come by and wanted to speak with me."

"He should be here soon. That man would be late to his own funeral." Maddox cackled. "But here, let me introduce you around to some folks."

"Thanks."

Maddox took her around, and she was already forgetting names. They soon ended up in the adjoining room where the bar was. She found Carson standing at the bar sipping on a drink while chatting with the bartender.

"There you are," she murmured, arriving at his side.

"I figured I'd let you mingle and do your thing." He chuckled. He brought her to his side and dropped a kiss on her forehead.

"Carson, this is Maddox Vaughn. Maddox, this is my boyfriend, Carson Brooks," she made quick introductions.

Carson had skipped out earlier before they could be introduced.

"Nice to meet you, man." Maddox shook Carson's hand. "As I was telling your girl, we need more women in country."

"I'll drink to that." Carson tipped his glass to Maddox.

Demi knew Carson was a big country fan. All of the music he played was nothing but country and some rock.

"You're trying to cross over to country?" a deep raspy voice chimed in behind Demi.

She turned around and found country music legend Vincent Norwood eyeing her. He had a reputation of being an asshole and a crazed lunatic. He had gotten in trouble one time too many. It was a wonder he still even had a label to back him.

"Um, yeah, I am," Demi replied.

Carson stiffened next to her. He knocked back the rest of his drink and sat the empty glass down on the counter. He turned and faced Vincent, his gaze locked on the country star.

"What you crossing over for? Why can't you stay singing your own music? We don't need the likes of you messing up what we've created." Vincent guzzled his shot, slamming the glass on the bar. "I'll take another one." He motioned to the bartender.

"I'm sorry. Did anyone ask you for your opinion?" Carson snapped. His voice was low, a half growl.

"Carson, baby. It's okay." Demi rested a hand on Carson's chest.

His gaze didn't waver from Vincent's.

"Do you know who I am?" Vincent taunted.

Demi shut her eyes. That was the wrong thing to stay. Carson wasn't one of his LA lackeys, running errands for a random celebrity.

Carson had bragged how he and his brothers didn't start fights but were good at ending them.

She just prayed this wasn't the night he started an altercation.

"Hey, I'm sure he didn't mean it the way he said," Maddox interjected.

"No, I want to hear what he meant," Carson snarled, gently moving Demi out of the way.

Demi glanced around in search of Lester or Kevin.

Neither were in sight.

They were drawing a small crowd.

"Do you know who I am, boy?" Vincent stood from his seat at the bar.

Oh shit.

Did he really just call Carson *boy*?

Carson heard nothing but the threat directed toward his woman. He didn't care who the asshole was. The man could be the fucking President of the United States and he'd still want to punch him in the face.

He was going to give Demi the respect she deserved.

It had nothing to do with what she wanted to sing. This asshat had nothing to do with their conversation and had nothing to do with what Demi decided to do as an artist.

Carson wasn't going to let anyone speak ill of Demi while in his presence.

And this fucker had the audacity to call him *boy*?

Fuck this.

"First of all, I couldn't care less who you are," Carson bit out through gritted teeth. He recognized the guy, but that didn't mean that he could just talk any kind of way he wanted. "You don't get to say what she can or cannot sing."

"All I'm saying is her people have plenty—"

"Be very careful of the next words you speak." Carson was seeing red. His hands balled into tight fists as he stared the man down.

Her people?

What the fuck was that supposed to mean?

"Why don't you take a walk?" Maddox suggested, eyeing Carson and Vincent.

"For what? Me and this fucknut are just having a conversation," Carson said.

"Carson, baby. It's fine." Demi moved to his side, resting her hand on his forearm. "We can leave now. I'll set something up with Austin later."

"We aren't going anywhere." Carson sneered. He peeled her hand off his forearm and pushed her behind him again. "Not until this son of a bitch apologizes."

"What are you going to do, make me?" Vincent snorted.

The couple of guys with him chuckled. Vincent

stood from his seat and got closer to Carson. The men with him also stood, their smiles fading.

Carson eyed the three of them. He had a few inches on all of them and was solid muscle, while their builds were questionable.

He'd had worse odds before and wasn't afraid of the three of them.

"You don't want that," Carson murmured. He scraped a hand along the side of his face. He was going to give this asshole one last chance to apologize to Demi. "Where I'm from, men don't go poking their noses in other people's conversations, or disrespecting women. Now apologize."

He ignored the crowd they were drawing.

"Move on, boy." Vincent jabbed his fingers into Carson's chest. "I don't give a shit where you are from. We don't need the likes of her singing our music."

Carson exploded.

His fist landed right on Vincent's face. The satisfying crunch of his nose breaking would have pleased Carson, but he was too far gone.

All hell broke loose.

Screams filled the air. Carson didn't have time to think of where Demi was. He sent up a prayer that Lester had her.

The three men tried to converge on him, but Carson was very skilled in the fine art of whipping ass. This would have been a great day to have his brothers with him, but he didn't need them.

It had been a while since he'd been in a good ol' fight.

Vincent and his friends weren't the fighting type, leaving Carson slightly disappointed.

One tried to grab Carson, but he was able to twist his arm and yank the guy to him, punching him in the solar plexus. He fell forward, just in time for Carson to bring his knee up, connecting with his face. He dropped to the floor, cursing, holding his nose.

The third guy grasped Carson from behind in a bear hug. He fell backward, using his weight to his advantage and trapping the guy against the bar. His hold loosened slightly on Carson.

Vincent cursed and rushed to Carson with his arm cocked back.

Carson brought his feet up, kicking Vincent in the chest, sending him flying to the floor. People scattered, screams echoing around them. Out of the corner of his eye, he clocked security making their way to them.

Carson spun around, sending a left jab into the

face of the dark-haired guy behind him. Carson blocked his halfhearted return of a punch, sending a right hook into the dude's stomach.

"Break this shit up," a voice growled.

Two men snagged Carson by the arms and dragged him away.

"You broke my fucking nose," Vincent hollered, standing from the floor. Blood marred his once crisp white shirt.

Other men in black shirts with security splashed across the front stepped over to them. One pushed Vincent back to keep him from coming forward.

"Let him go," Carson growled. He wasn't done with the son of a bitch. Carson's chest was rising and falling fast. He was just getting started beating an apology out of the bastard. The damn guards just had to come and ruined his fun.

The room was now cleared out and was flooded with security.

"I got him. He's with me." Lester appeared next to the security guards dragging Carson away.

"Get him out of here, Lester," the one on Carson's right said. He turned his glare to Carson. "I don't want to see you again tonight."

"I hope you're kicking that asshole and his

friends out, too," Carson snapped. He shook them off him.

"Cool it, man," Lester muttered. He took Carson by the arm and guided him out of the room and down the hall. "I don't know what the hell set you off, but Vincent Norwood is a royal jerk."

"Yeah, I learned," Carson muttered.

"I used to work for him, years ago. He's a piece of work. I would have paid money to see you kick his ass."

They exited the house to find the majority of the party attendees standing outside. He scanned the yard and didn't see her anywhere.

"Where is Demi?" Carson asked. He glanced down at his throbbing knuckles, finding them bruised and busted. He grimaced. It wasn't the first time he'd experienced this. Ice and some Tylenol would help.

"Safe. Kevin put her in the truck."

Carson was satisfied with that admission. He noticed one thing.

No cop cars.

"Why aren't the cops being called?" Carson asked, following Lester.

"Parties with this type of clientele won't want the police showing up. It's bad for business unless someone got shot or killed or something." Lester pointed to the dark SUV that was parked at the edge of the roundabout. The engine was idling. "Now, I can't say this won't be kept off the internet. I'm sure people are all uploading their videos."

Carson cursed. In this day and age, everyone recorded everything.

He jogged toward the truck and opened the back door.

"Carson!" Demi cried out. She moved over to allow him to crawl in with her. "Are you okay?"

"Yeah." He grimaced, shutting the door behind him.

Lester ran around to the front and hopped in the passenger seat. Kevin put the vehicle in drive and took off.

"I'm so sorry." Carson turned to Demi. He hadn't really thought of how this could affect her. She was there to network with people, and here he was, ruining the entire party by fist fighting.

"Why are you apologizing?" She shook her head and scooted closer to him. "You were defending my honor."

"Believe me when I say Vincent had it coming," Lester said. "No one stands up to him, they just let him spout off at the mouth without repercussions. I just wished I could have seen when you first swung on him."

"He's one hell of a jerk." Kevin shook his head while guiding the truck into traffic.

"I don't want to ruin—"

"You aren't," Demi cut him off. She took his hand and assessed his bruised knuckles. "Vincent Norwood deserved to be punched in the face. I just wished I could have been the one doing it."

Her voice ended on a sexy growl.

Carson grinned at his bloodthirsty woman.

"Calm down, my little Xenia warrior." He snickered.

She leaned against him and snuggled into his embrace. "Don't worry about a thing."

"Shouldn't I be comforting you?" he asked, glancing down at her.

"You don't think I didn't expect a bit of pushback to switching to country?" She sat back slightly but still held on to his hand. "There have been a few singers of color who have been successful at singing country. Why? I have no clue. It's not like black folks don't listen to it, because we do."

Carson gazed down at Demi and fell more in love with her. She was brave and not afraid to face adversary. He would never know what it would feel like to be judged or discriminated because of the color of his skin, but there was one thing he did know.

It wasn't going to happen on his watch.

DEMI WALKED OUT OF THE MASTER EN SUITE and found Carson still asleep in bed. She tied her robe closed and tiptoed out of the room. She closed the door softly. She spun around and bit back a scream.

"Sorry," Jaimie whispered, standing behind her.

"You scared the crap out of me." Demi chuckled.

"Sorry. I was just coming to get you." Jaimie grabbed her arm and practically dragged her behind her.

They went down the stairs and headed toward the family room.

"Can I get coffee first?" Demi groaned.

"You won't need coffee after you see this." Jaimie let her go and waved for her to follow. The television was on the local news.

"What's wrong?" Demi murmured, slowing down. She took in grainy videos of the party they'd attended last night. "Oh no."

"Wait. Listen to what they are saying." Jaimie

motioned for her to sit on the couch. Her sister flopped down on the loveseat and folded her legs underneath her.

Demi bit her lip; her breath caught in her throat.

Last night had been wild. Carson had gone from laid-back cowboy to barroom brawler in two seconds when Vincent had started talking his racist nonsense.

He had joked about fighting, but boy, could he. He'd handled those three men as if he did it every day. She had stood frozen in place watching him before she was knocked out of the way.

"Welcome back. I'm Hope Wu, and here is you early morning news." She turned to face another camera. "Last night's partying in Beverly Hills ended with excitement. A brawl broke out at Grammy Award Winning songwriter Austin Keller's home last night. The fight was between Vincent Norwood and the boyfriend of Demi Day, Carson Brooks."

Video of Carson and Vincent arguing came on the screen. She watched the rerun of Carson placing her behind him. Her heart fluttered at the move.

He was protecting her.

"Apparently, what they were arguing over has landed Vincent in very hot water," the co-anchor, Bill Shield, said. He stared into the camera with a serious expression. "The country star has been known to make racist statements over the years, and it would seem his team is finally done with him."

"Oh my," Demi murmured. She was completely captivated by the news broadcast.

They showed old footage of Vincent stumbling from his car, obviously inebriated. He'd come home, and his neighbors, who were black, were having a small gathering. Vincent was recorded shouting racial slurs and expletives at them.

Demi remembered this video. It had been spread all over the news, but Vincent had not received any reprimand about it. He had released a recorded apology, and that was it. There had been boycotts for his music to be pulled, but the industry continued to back him.

"His booking agent has resigned, his label has suspended him for the moment, and his upcoming performance at the Coca-Cola Music Festival has been canceled," Hope said. She shook her head and turned to face Bill. "This, I have to admit, is long overdue."

"Am I dreaming?" Demi whispered.

"Girl, I've been glued to this television since I first woke up. They have been talking about you, Carson, and Vincent all morning."

Demi barely heard what her sister was saying.

"And to top it off, Vincent's music has been pulled from country radio. It looks as if he will finally have to face the consequences of his actions." Bill sighed.

Demi picked up the remote and changed the channel. She stopped on another that had video of her and Carson walking the red carpet.

"You two make one hot couple," Jaimie murmured.

"Thanks." She smiled, reaching up to tuck her hair behind her ear. She bit her lip, thinking of last night when they had arrived back from the party. She had practically jumped Carson's bones. It was something about watching her man fight to defend her honor that was a complete turn-on.

"Welcome back to the early morning edition of the *Hotlist*. I'm Amber Towns," Amber announced.

"And I'm Jamal Brown," Jamal said. "We finally know who the mystery man is who Demi Day has been snuggling up with."

"Our Demi went to Colorado and came back with a good ol' cowboy." Amber laughed. She faced Jamal. "And a super-hot one who is loaded."

Demi rolled her eyes. She didn't care about

Carson's financials. He could be poor and she would still love him.

"Hey, what's going on?" Carson mumbled. He walked into the room, tugging a white t-shirt on, hiding his perfectly sculpted abdomen. He had on gray sweatpants and padded over to her barefoot. He sat on the couch and hauled her onto his lap.

"Morning," she murmured, turning and planting a quick kiss to his lips. His hair was standing up on end. She smiled and reached up to smooth it down. "Sleep well?"

His lips spread into his sexy crooked grin. He pulled her to him, his lips brushing her ear. She bit back a moan at the feeling of his erection resting against her bottom.

"If you would have stayed around longer, you could have found out."

"Okay, you two." Jaimie groaned. She held hands up to block the sight of them. "I would say get a room, but this is your damn house, sis."

Demi kissed Carson again, unable to resist him.

"Later," he whispered. Carson's gray eyes darkened.

Her core clenched in anticipation of what his promise would mean.

"What's going on?" he asked.

"Apparently, Vincent is finally getting in trouble for his racist ways," Demi said. She quickly caught him up on what the news channels were sharing.

"I can't believe he's been allowed to go this long with that type of attitude," Carson muttered.

"Well, it looks like because of everything going on in this country today, all of that is about to change," Demi replied. She turned back to the television, wrapped up in Carson's embrace.

"Demi not only found herself a wealthy rancher, but she put that fine man in a suit and made him walk the red carpet with her at the Writers' Guild awards ceremony. Our girl Demi has great taste in men." Amber winked at the camera. "Makes me want to travel to Colorado to see who else they've got hidden away there."

Carson snorted.

"Demi, there's still a chance, right?" Jamal looked into the camera with big pleading eyes.

"Not happening, buddy," Carson growled, his hold tightening on Demi.

"You don't have anything to worry about." Demi petted his hand. She turned her head toward him and grinned. "You have my heart."

"Oh, puh-lease." Jaime groaned and rolled her eyes.

"Don't be jealous, sis." Demi laughed. She wrapped her arms around Carson's neck and kissed his cheek. "She's just jealous," she whispered into his ear.

"Whatever." Jaimie shook her head, a grin on her lips. She grew still, staring at Carson. "You don't have a single brother hidden anywhere?"

Carson barked a laugh. "Sorry, Jaimie. There's only three of us. But I do have a few cousins who are available."

❧ 24 ❧

"Let me hear the playback," Demi said, pulling her wireless earphones off her ears, resting them around her neck. She glanced over at her sound engineer, Cary. She walked outside the booth and took a seat in the chair next to him.

"Got it," he replied. He hit a few buttons before music flowed from the speakers. Her voice came in, husky and perfect.

She swayed to the music. The song she had written was flawless.

"That's sounds good," Jaimie said from her seat.

Demi spun the chair around and took in Carson sitting beside her sister. They had spent the entire week together. She wanted to bring him into her world.

"What do you think?" she asked, focusing on Carson who grinned.

"Any time I hear you sing, I'm blown away," he admitted. He leaned back on the couch and shrugged. He twisted his baseball cap around, putting the brim facing backwards. "I'm the last person to ask, though. It all sounds good."

She was happy to share this part of herself with him. They were coming to know each other so well. Each day they were together, she found herself falling more in love with him. He was patient with her in the studio, never complained. It was comforting for him to be there. She liked having him watch her work.

When she was in the booth, she sang for him. The words she had written, most had been because of him. The emotions she had put into her romantic ballads were for him.

Having him there helped her channel her emotions into the songs.

The album was shaping up quite nicely. She was excited for what she had already. They were planning the launch. She had to decide on which song was going to be the lead single.

She had to pick the perfect song.

A girl only had one chance to make a good impression with her new audience, and she couldn't mess it up.

"I think we need to do the hook again," Reno, her producer, suggested.

"That's what I was thinking." She turned back around and tapped out a few commands on her laptop that rested on the mixing desk.

"You need to go down a little lower." Reno sang the hook, dropping to a lower note.

"I think you're right. Let me go back in there." She stood but then paused at the sound of a phone ringing. She looked around and saw it was hers. Picking it up from the desk, she didn't recognize the number. "Hello?"

"Hi, is this Demi?" an unfamiliar voice asked.

"Yes, it is."

"Hey, it's Austin Keller," he announced.

Demi spun around and met the curious gaze of her sister. She mouthed Austin's name. Jaimie's eyes grew round.

"Hi, Austin. How are you?" She took a seat again.

Austin was one of the biggest songwriters there was. He didn't come cheap, but it would be an honor to work with him. They were supposed to speak about working together at his party, but due to Vincent, they'd never got the chance.

"I'm good. First of all, I want to apologize for what happened at my house."

"You don't have to apologize."

"I do. I got caught up with the awards and stopped by a friend's house before going to my party. Had I been there, Vincent wouldn't have been there."

"Really?" she asked.

"I refused to work with that jackass. He crashed my party, wanting to meet with me. I don't even know how he got past security."

"Wow." She was left speechless.

"If you get a chance, tell that boyfriend of yours I said thank you for putting Vincent in his place."

Demi laughed. That's all she'd been hearing. Until Carson, no one'd had the balls to stand up to Vincent.

This was proving to be a very costly error for him. Demi hoped he learned from his mistakes.

"I will certainly do that." She winked at Carson. "What can I do for you, Austin?"

Demi tried to appear calm and collected. On the inside, her anxiety was through the roof. She had been wanting to work with Austin for years. She prayed he was calling her with good news.

"Well, we were supposed to connect so we could talk about collaborating. I would love to work with you on your first country album. I know you are going to take the world by storm."

She danced in place, happy about his offer. The man was a genius when it came to writing hit songs. Together, they were guaranteed a chart-topping song.

"I'd love to work with you," she breathed. Demi's cheeks were growing sore from her grinning so much. All of her dreams were seriously coming true.

"Perfect. Let's set something up."

She disconnected the call and jumped up from her chair, dancing crazy.

They all laughed at her antics.

"Austin's on board!" she shouted.

"Oh, yeah!" Jaimie danced along with her to their imaginary music.

Demi danced over to Carson and plopped down on his lap. She leaned down and pressed a kiss to his lips.

Everything was turning out to be perfect.

DEMI SAT ON HER TERRACE, SOAKING UP THE sun while she wrote. Her creativity had been flowing. She had lost count of the songs she had written.

Some were too personal to share.

She'd been up since sunrise, working on material. She and Austin had set up a date for next week for them to sit down and talk about the direction of her album and brainstorm. Out of all the songs she'd recorded, she'd only approved a few so far for the final cut of the album.

"How did I know I'd find you out here." Carson stepped out the door.

Her mouth went dry at the sight of him. Dressed in jeans and a t-shirt, he was the epitome of sexiness.

"Just working." She shrugged, watching him saunter over to the banister.

He leaned against it and gazed upon the view.

Placing her notebook down on the table beside her, she stood and walked over to join him.

"Are you enjoying yourself?" she asked. In between meetings and the studio, she ensured she was able to show him around LA. He was on vacation while visiting with her, and she wanted to make sure he was able to sightsee.

"I am." He wrapped an arm around her waist and

drew her to him. "Anywhere you are, I'm going to enjoy."

Demi chuckled and leaned into him. "You are just saying that."

"I'm serious. LA isn't for me, but it's nice to visit." He turned his attention to her backyard.

It was perfectly manicured and had a gorgeous pool. Hakim was currently playing in the water with a friend of his. Their laughter floated through the air.

"That's how I feel." It was amazing how much they were alike. She'd always said the same thing about the city. No matter how long she'd live here, she would always prefer the country to this crowded metropolitan area.

"Well, it just so happens that I have a place out in the middle of a ranch. It's quiet, plenty of land and open skies," he murmured.

"Really? I may have to come visit and check it out."

"Why don't you move in with me there?"

They froze in place, staring at each other. She swallowed hard. As fast as their relationship was moving, she should have been taken aback by the request.

But Carson was a man who she would be a fool to let go.

"There's only so much I can do from there." She sighed. It was a tempting offer, but there wasn't any way she could record. "I would still have to fly back and forth."

"I know, but at least you can have a home away from home." Carson cupped her cheek, rubbing her skin softly with his thumb. "With me."

Carson Brooks was a very persuasive man.

"With you?"

She rested against him, his hard erection pressing on her stomach.

"Yup. Just think. Waking up in our bed, you on your back, me tasting what's in between your thighs."

Demi trembled, imagining what he was describing. Moisture collected at the apex of her thighs. She blinked hard, the memories of her riding his tongue coming to mind. The man had a wicked way with her body.

"Carson," she whimpered. Memories of him devouring her pussy had her grasping at his t-shirt. "You shouldn't be saying things like that."

"Why not?" He cocked an eyebrow up. "You know you like it."

"Too much."

He leaned down and captured her lips in a

sizzling kiss she could feel all the way down to her toes. She skated her hands up along his chest, settling at the base of his neck.

The shrill ringing of her phone broke the moment. She drew away and glanced over at her phone on the table. She contemplated ignoring the call, but she knew she couldn't. There was too much going on that she was going to have to answer.

"Hold that thought." She walked over and snagged her phone. She slid her finger along the glass screen to answer. "Hello?"

"Is this Demi?" a voice rasped.

"It is. May I ask who's calling?"

Carson came over to her and took a seat on the chaise she had abandoned. He pulled her down onto his lap. His erection pushed against her bottom. She glanced over at him with wide eyes.

He had the nerve to wink at her.

"It's Vince. Vincent Norwood."

Demi grew tense. Carson nudged her, obviously sensing the change in her body language.

"What's wrong?" he whispered. He stiffened as he waited for her to reply.

"Vincent. How did you get my number?" she asked.

Carson snorted.

"I hope you don't mind me being too forward. My ex-agent knows your publicist and was able to get your number."

Demi closed her eyes briefly. She was going to have to have a chat with Rowan about giving out her phone number.

"Okay. Well, what do you want?" She hardened her voice, not trusting the racist piece of shit.

"Look, I know what I said the other day was wrong. I want the opportunity to say I'm sorry."

Demi grew quiet.

He wanted to apologize?

"You want to say sorry?" She glanced over at Carson whose eyebrows were propped up high.

A slight chuckle escaped him.

"I'm in some pretty hot water and wanted to publicly make amends for my behavior. But before I do that, I wanted to first apologize to you."

"What do you have in mind?" She reached out and entwined her fingers with Carson's who was listening quietly to her half of the conversation.

"Why don't we meet for coffee today. Say in an hour?" Vincent suggested.

Demi glanced down at her watch. She didn't have to be at the studio until later.

"An hour would be fine. Where?"

Vincent picked a local coffee shop that she was familiar with. They disconnected the call, and she turned to Carson.

"What did that fucknut want?" Carson asked.

Demi held back a chuckle at his nickname for Vincent.

"He wanted to meet for coffee so he could officially apologize to me."

"Well, I wonder where he got that notion from," Carson said sarcastically.

"You're coming with me, right?"

"You just try to stop me."

Demi placed a call to Lester to notify him she now had an appointment. When she was in LA, she didn't go anywhere without him. Within twenty minutes, they were getting into the SUV with Lester driving them to their destination.

Demi had dressed casually and kept her makeup light. For this, she didn't need to be dressed up. Pushing up her big black sunglasses to the top of her head, she faced Carson.

"No fighting," she warned.

"As long as he doesn't talk out the side of his neck, we're good." He shrugged.

"Don't worry, Demi. I'll be there, too," Lester announced.

The ride to the cafe was short, and soon they were stopping in front of it.

Lester came around and opened the back door for her. She stepped from the truck and pulled her glasses down to cover her eyes. They helped to keep people from recognizing her.

Carson exited behind her and took her hand. He led her into the small café and stopped by the hostess station.

"Hello." Demi came to stand at Carson's side. "We're here to meet a friend, Vincent Norwood."

"Oh, yes. Right this way." The hostess motioned for them to follow her.

Carson towed her behind him as they navigated through the small restaurant. The hostess led them to an outside patio where Vincent was sitting alone.

"Here you go." The young woman waved to the table. "Your server should be here momentarily."

She scurried off before Demi could even offer her thanks.

"Thank you for joining me on such a short notice." Vincent nodded to the both of them. He stood and motioned for them to take a seat.

Carson pulled out her chair and assisted her, then he claimed the empty one next to hers.

Vincent glanced nervously at Carson and sat back down.

"You're welcome," Demi responded politely.

The waitress arrived and took their drink orders before disappearing.

Demi and Carson sat quietly staring at Vincent who appeared haggard. His beard was growing in, while his clothes looked as if he'd slept in them.

"I don't want to keep you too long. I'm sure you're a busy woman," Vincent began. He shoved a hand through his hair and sighed. "I'm going to start off and tell you that I haven't had a drop of alcohol since that night."

Demi glanced over at Carson, then turned her attention back to Vincent.

"Okay," Demi replied.

"I drink. A lot. Not that it's any excuse. I'm going to get help for it." Vincent took a sip of the water that was sitting in front of him. "Everything that has been happening to me is because of me. I'm a man and will deal with the repercussions of my words and actions. I am asking you for forgiveness for my inappropriate words."

Demi paused, staring at Vincent. He had been in the industry for years. She remembered watching him perform on television when she was a child.

"Not only did you hurt me, but you tried to suppress me as a black artist like so many others have done before you. Music is a beautiful way to share emotion, expressions, love, and experiences," Demi said. "And I should be able to do that."

"You're right." Vincent nodded.

"I was insulted and hurt by your words. You have been around long enough that I would have thought you would want to introduce more fans to the beauty of country music. It should be something shared with everyone, but you decided to say that we should stick to our own music. That was devastating coming from someone who many look up to."

The waitress came by and dropped off their drinks. Demi picked up her latte and sipped. It was really good, and she had to hold back her groan. She was too riled up at the moment and wanted to finish getting everything off her chest.

Carson quietly sat next to her, sipping on his large black coffee. His hand resting on her knee was comforting and lent her strength.

"What would you have me to do?" Vincent asked.

"Aside from the apology statement?" she asked.

He gave her nod.

She bit her lip and thought for a second on what

he could do to make up for all of his racist views. "Where do you live?"

"Nashville."

She glanced over at Carson who gave her a slight nod. An idea struck her at that moment. There was something Vincent could do that would be beneficial and show how dedicated he was to changing. It wouldn't be something that could take place overnight but would be worth it once he got it up and running.

"I want you to set up a charity to help inner city youths. A music program that is geared toward introducing all genres of music to children of color."

A pique of interest glimmered in Vincent's eyes. He sat back and took a healthy sip of his coffee. "That I can do. I've been hearing that a lot of the music programs in the urban areas have been cut."

"Then that will be all you would need to do." She sat up taller, proud of herself. Not only would he apologize publicly, but youngsters in Nashville would benefit from it. "And get help to stay sober."

He raised his mug in the air. Demi tipped hers to his in a toast to seal the deal.

Vincent turned his attention to Carson. "I need to apologize to you, too, but I don't want to do anything to warrant another one of your left hooks."

"Follow through with what you're promising, and you won't have to worry about me."

"I wish you didn't have to go," Demi murmured. She slid into bed and snuggled up under his arm. They had retired a little early since Carson had a flight to catch back to Colorado in the morning.

Carson brought her in closer, his arm resting around her waist.

"I have to go home. I can't stay here forever." He sighed. Carson bent down and kissed the top of her head. He breathed in her scent. She was fresh from the shower and smelled of jasmine. The rich, floral fragrance filled his senses.

"You smell good." He leaned over, inhaling deeply.

"You like it?" She grinned up at him. "It's one of

my shower creams I'll be launching. It's a deep moisturizer that helps keep skin toned and youthful-looking."

"Me likey." He ran a hand along her arm, finding her skin smooth and supple. She may be onto something.

His time in California had flown by. Now it was time for him to go back to Shady Springs. LA was okay, but it wasn't anywhere he would want to live.

Demi had been right. There were too many people. He needed the open land and fresh air. He was a country boy and was dying to get back on his horse and ride.

"I know." Demi pouted. She pushed up and rested her head on her hand. "I guess we will officially begin testing out this long-distance relationship."

It was something they had spoken about. They would be flying back and forth to see each other.

"My offer still stands." He had plenty of room in his house. He had built that home with a future family in mind. It was only him, so there were plenty of spare bedrooms available. He wanted her in Shady Springs permanently. There was no getting around her having to leave to go to LA for work, but at least her primary residence would be with him.

"You've made such a compelling argument."

"I know what I want." He reached over and cupped her face.

Demi took it and glanced at it. His knuckles were still red and had scabbed over.

"Does it still hurt?" she asked, softly kissing his hand.

"Not really." He flexed it, feeling only slight pain. He'd busted his knuckles up worse than this in the past.

"I really appreciate you." She kissed his lips.

Carson cupped the back of her neck, holding her in place.

She drew away from him and stared into his eyes. Carson couldn't believe he had landed such a beautiful, smart, and amazing woman.

"I'll always protect what's mine," he murmured. He had been afraid his temper would have caused issues with her, but instead, it appeared to do the opposite.

Wade and Parker had called him by the next morning after the fight, busting his balls. They rode him for leaving them to go fight in another state. They always fought together.

How dare he?

But really, it was his elder brothers making sure they didn't need to come to California to help him.

Had he said the word, the two of them would have been on the next flight to LA to come stand by his side.

That's how the Brooks brothers operated.

"I like the sound of that," she whispered.

He pulled her into his embrace. He didn't want to leave her but he had to. It would only be a short while before she would be joining him in Shady Springs.

She was his, and he wanted to take the time to show her in every possible way he knew how.

"Just think. We can remodel the basement and put a studio there for you to work out of the house." He wasn't about bribing his woman to entice her to come live with him.

She grinned at him.

Carson continued on. "The backyard has an amazing patio where you can write while looking out a nature. You want to get away from the city, right? We have plenty of land, local festivals, we can go cow tipping—"

"Oh my god!" Demi burst out laughing.

Carson hugged her tight. He rolled them over to where he braced himself over her. She widened her legs to allow him to rest in the valley of her thighs. His cock strained against his boxer briefs at the warmth that met him.

They both released a deep-seated groan.

"What's so funny?" He bent down and dropped a kiss on her lips.

"Cow tipping?"

"I own plenty of them."

"What else do you have back in Colorado for me?" she breathed. Her dark eyes widened as he ground his pelvis to hers.

"Anything you want." His lips brushed hers. His hands slid underneath them and tugged on her tiny cami. It did nothing to hide her body from him. It was pointless for her to even have put it on. He pulled it over her head and tossed it onto the floor.

Her soft, supple body was made for him. Her nipples beaded into tight little brown buds. He licked his lips, ready to draw them into his mouth.

"What if all I want is you?" Demi wrapped her arms around his neck.

Carson paused, staring down into her beautiful eyes. There wasn't anything he wouldn't do for this woman. She was everything he could have dreamed of. She was smart, level-headed, had a big heart, a silly personality, and a sexy body.

Carson rested his forehead on hers, feeling nothing but love for her.

"I love you." He had never said those words to any woman beside his mother. The sensations floating around his chest were raw and wild.

"I love you, too."

Their hands tore at the clothing they both wore. Once naked, he parted Demi's thighs and thrust home.

A groan rumbled from him at the sensation of her silky wet heat surrounding him. Demi's soft moans echoed through the air, driving the desire for her inside him to a level beyond belief.

He hips moved faster, his cock slipping deeper inside her.

He pounded into her with a reckless abandon, unable to get enough of her. Demi's nails scraped along his back, marking him.

"Carson," she moaned. Demi's head was thrown back, her face filled with ecstasy.

Carson loved when she let loose and took her pleasure from him. He lowered his head to the crook of her neck, pressing hot kisses along her skin.

"What is the answer, Demi?" he rasped. He nipped her ear. He surged froward and held himself still. It took all of his control to not move. He was buried so far inside her, he didn't know where she began or where he ended.

He was going to get his answer.

Her walls clenched around him. She opened her eyes, a sexy smile gracing her lips.

"Yes, Carson. I'll move in with you." Her giggle filled the air. She tugged his head down to her and pressed her lips to his. Her soft lips commanded his.

It took his breath away how sweet and sensual it was.

"Good." He tore his mouth from hers. He lifted her leg and braced it on his arm. He pulled back before thrusting forward hard, eliciting a gasp from her. "You won't regret it, superstar."

EPILOGUE

Four months later

She had done it. Completed her first country album, *Country at Heart*. Her blood, sweat, and tears had gone into the making of this record. She had been blown away with the amount of support she had gained from the industry. Her first single, the duet with Chad, was sitting at the top of the charts.

Butterflies filled her as she glanced around the living room of Carson's—their—home. She now spent more time in Colorado than she did in California.

There was just something about this place that enticed her.

Carson.

She didn't think she could be more in love with him than she was. He was the perfect man for her.

She had no doubts about taking the leap with him. He was everything she could ever ask for in a man.

She had kept her house in LA, where Jaimie and Hakim used it as their primary home. She used it as a crashing pad when she was in town.

With Carson's help, they had done the first phase of renovations on their home. Her brand-new studio was beautiful and very state-of-the-art. When she'd moved in, he had given her free rein to help make his home, their home.

The family room held their family and friends. Carson's family was spread out, mingling with hers.

Her parents had flown in along with her brother, Frankie. Her family had fallen in love with Carson just as fast as she had.

Frankie was currently in deep conversation with Parker. When she'd walked past them, all she'd caught were the words 'bull riding' and she kept moving. Her brother was a big fan of the sport and had even recognized Parker.

"All right, everyone." Demi cleared her throat.

She held her phone that was connected with the speaker system.

Maddy sat on the couch with little Gracie. The new addition was the apple of her father's and uncles' eyes. Demi pitied any boy who dared tried to date her. The Brooks men, including Tyler, were very protective of her.

Joy, Wade's fiancée, was due any moment and posted up on the couch next to Maddy.

Her team was there with her.

Rowan, Janet, Lester, Cary, were all in the house.

The doorbell rang.

"I'll get it," Carson volunteered.

All eyes were now on her.

"Thank you for coming to share with me the first listen of my latest album. It means so much to me that all of my closest friends and family could be here with me."

Applause went around the room.

In two days, she would be flying out to LA for the official listening party where all of the industry was invited to hear the record.

"You know I already love you." Maddy chuckled.

"That means so much." Demi winked at her. She gazed around the room and blew a kiss to her father who was deep in conversation with Carson's dad, Jonah.

This was a night she wouldn't forget.

"I know you weren't going to start without me?" Nina's voice sounded in the doorway.

She and Sid walked in. Sid was carrying their daughter, Savannah. The wide-eyed two-year-old was cautiously looking around the room. She wrapped an arm around her father's neck, showing no intent of getting down from his embrace.

"Nina!" Demi rushed over and hugged her friend. "I thought you were going to come to the LA event."

"I am, but I wanted to be with you tonight. This is the better party." Nina hugged her.

"Do you want some wine or a drink? We have a bar over there." Demi waved her hand over to where Wade and Jaimie were standing chatting.

Nina grew bashful and leaned into Demi. "I'm pregnant."

"Really?" Demi squealed. She hugged her friend again. "Congratulations."

"Yeah, Sid apparently wants to keep me barefoot and pregnant." Nina rolled her eyes, a wide grin spreading across her face.

"Whatever." Sid snorted.

"Please have a seat. We have plenty of room."

Carson walked in with a few extra folding chairs to put around the room.

Love filled Demi as she gazed at their family. Everything was going just as she had prayed.

Her cosmetic line had launched with her mother at the helm of the development team. The products flew off the shelves and were sold out everywhere. They were having to increase production just to meet the demands. Day Beauty was quickly becoming a household name.

Who would have thought that a bright-eyed girl from Waco, Texas, would be running a cosmetics empire and singing her favorite kind of songs for all of the world to hear.

Her former label regretted letting her go. With her impending record expected to sell like crazy, it was their loss but Demi's gain.

"All right, baby. Let's put them out of their misery." Carson came to her side and wrapped an arm around her waist and guided her back in front of everyone. "They are here to hear some great tunes."

"Hear, hear!" Rowan shouted. "Stop teasing us, woman."

Demi giggled and pulled up the app on her phone that would connect with the speakers she'd had put around the house.

"Okay, okay!" Demi held her up hand. She looked around the room, grinning. "Now just know, I'm an artist and I'm sensitive about my work."

"Just hit 'play' already," Maddy pleaded.

"But before you do…" Carson coughed. He dropped down on one knee and lifted a small velvet black box in his hand.

Demi froze.

Laughter went up in the air. Her gaze connected with his smoky-gray eyes. Tears blurred her vision.

"What are you doing?" she whispered, watching him take her hand in his.

She glanced up and saw her parents smiling and nodding, giving their approval. Frankie and Jaimie were clapping along with everyone else.

Nina was standing recording everything on her phone.

Now it all made sense why Nina preferred to be here.

Carson had waited until their entire families were together for not only her big moment to share with them the album she had been working so hard on, but for them to witness something else.

"Demi, there is no one else in the world that I want to spend my days with. You blew into my life and filled it with so much joy. I need you," Carson said. "Will you marry me?"

The tears slowly made their way down her cheeks.

Demi was so choked up with emotion, all she could do was nod.

"What does that mean, superstar?" He laughed.

"Yes!" she cried out.

Cheers exploded at her answer.

He slid the gorgeous diamond ring onto her finger and stood. He brought her in and claimed her lips in the sweetest of kisses.

Surrounded by friends and family, the night couldn't get any more perfect.

Months ago, she'd traveled to the country to get away, not knowing she would find her heart.

Dear reader,

Thank you for taking the time to read Country at Heart. I hope you loved reading Carson and Demi's book. I had so much fun with them that I was sad to see their book end.

Now for me to keep this series going, I need to hear you say it in the reviews! We have a few hands we can give stories!

Warm wishes,

Peyton Banks

COWBOY, TAKE ME AWAY
BLAZING EAGLE RANCH 4

He's a broken cowboy in need of the love from a good woman…

Stan Larsen had trust issues. His ex-wife had done a number on him, so he threw himself into his work on the Blazing Eagle ranch. Hard back-breaking labor was just what he needed to erase the memories of her deception.

Maybe relationships weren't for him.

Until he met her.

Nasia Henry blew into his life like a deadly cattle stampede. Her smile and laughter brightened his days, making him feel something he once thought was lost. She filled his every thought and had him anticipating the future.

It all appeared too good to be true.

Then his past returned, reminding him of all the things he tried to forget.

But could he shake his past and trust again?

The next book in the Blazing Eagle Ranch is available now!

ABOUT THE AUTHOR

USA TODAY bestselling author, Peyton Banks, is the alter ego of a city girl who is a romantic at heart. Her mornings consist of coffee and daydreaming up the next steamy romance book ideas. She loves spinning romantic tales of hot alpha males and the women they love. Make sure you check her out!

Sign up for Peyton's Newsletter to find out the latest releases, giveaways and news! Visit www.peyton banks.com/newsletter to sign up!

Want to know the latest about Peyton Banks? Follow her online:

ALSO BY PEYTON BANKS

<u>Current Free Short Story</u>

Summer Escape

<u>Book Boyfriend Dating Agency</u>

Surgeon Book Boyfriend

<u>Silver Creek Ranch (Shared World)</u>

Wrangling Her Cowboy

<u>Lunchtime Chronicles (Peyton's)</u>

Polish Boy

Thick & Beefy

Rich & Decadent

<u>The Keith Brothers</u>

Mr. Hotness

Mr. Arrogant

<u>Blazing Eagle Ranch Series</u>

Back in the Saddle

Knockin' the Boots

Roping a Cowboy

Country at Heart

Cowboy, Take Me Away

Hard to Forget

<u>Special Weapons & Tactics Series</u>

Dirty Tactics (Special Weapons & Tactics 1)

Dirty Ballistics (Special Weapons & Tactics 2)

Dirty Operations (Special Weapons & Tactics 3)

Dirty Alliance (Special Weapons & Tactics 4)

Dirty Justice (Special Weapons & Tactics 5)

Dirty Trust (Special Weapons & Tactics 6)

Dirty Secrets (Special Weapons & Tactics 7)

Dirty Ultimatum (Special Weapons & Tactics 8)

<u>SWAT boxset, books 1-3</u>

<u>Trust & Honor Series (BWWM)</u>

Dallas

Dalton

<u>A Langdale Christmas</u>

The Christmas Secret

The Christmas Wish

The Christmas Gift

<u>Interracial Romances (BWWM)</u>

Pieces of Me

Hard Love

Retain Me

Silent Deception

<u>African American Romance</u>

Breaking The Rules

<u>Mafia Romance</u>

Unexpected Allies (The Tokhan Bratva 1)